Chance Encounter

by

Martha O'Sullivan

ISBN: 978-1-7367667-1-2

Chance Encounter

Cover by Charmaine Ross

Formatting by coversbykaren.com

To my daughters, Megan and Erin.
The most important thing I'll ever be is your mother.

The Chances Trilogy
By Martha O'Sullivan

Second Chance
Chance Encounter
Last Chance

Christmas in Tahoe (Coming in 2022)

Visit marthaosullivan.com for summaries, excerpts
and more.

CHAPTER ONE

IT HAD BEEN AGES since Delaney Richards had given a man a second thought, let alone a second look. But the pilot with the hints of gray at the temples of his chestnut-colored hair and smiling eyes had caught her unwitting attention. She watched him greet the oncoming passengers before his gaze found hers and lingered. Then, fever rushing to her cheeks, she pretended to contemplate the baggage handlers loading an adjacent plane. She felt his measured stare for a moment more before he turned away.

"Can I bring you a drink before takeoff?"

Delaney shifted her attention in the direction of the hospitable voice. "Water, please," she told the woman standing over her left shoulder. "Maybe a glass of red wine after takeoff."

The flight attendant shook her head in acknowledgement. "The aisle seat in your row isn't booked. Make yourself comfortable."

Delaney watched her return to the front of the plane and whisper something to the pilot.

Nodding in affirmation, he began retreating into the cockpit, but stopped short. His amber eyes met Delaney's and held briefly before he closed the door.

Shaking off the revery, Delaney opened her bag and retrieved her laptop. Being appointed interim vice-president had been a well-deserved yet unexpected promotion. And as luck would have it, she'd been thrown out of the frying pan and into the fire. Rebranding an investment firm with a reputation for tolerating sexual harassment in today's unsparing business climate had been a challenge to say the least. It had consumed her life for the last few months. Her presentation in San Francisco next week could ensure the position became permanent. And she planned to nail it.

She had no sooner brought up the opening slide of her PowerPoint presentation when the flight crew asked for everyone's attention to review the safety procedures. Like most of the passengers, Delaney immediately tuned them out. Until a resounding voice filled the cabin, abruptly pulling her out of work mode.

"Welcome to United Airlines Flight 1126 to San Francisco. This is your captain. We anticipate a smooth four-hour-and-change flight to SFO this evening. I'll update you along the way about our progress as well as point out any landmarks of note below. Thanks for flying with us. Enjoy the flight. We've got the best crew in the business with us tonight."

The next thing she knew, the flight attendant was back at her elbow again. "Not only do you have your row to yourself, but we've got the good

California wine tonight." She handed Delaney a glass and a cocktail napkin. "This must be your lucky day."

Delaney returned the smile as the other woman took her leave. Maybe it was. Maybe her luck was finally starting to change.

～

Even after twenty-plus years behind the stick Captain Mike Savoy never took a smooth landing for granted. Technical check behind him, he exchanged pleasantries with the flight crew before going out into the cabin to thank the passengers for their business.

But tonight his motivation was admittedly twofold. He wanted to see the woman in first-class again. She'd been asleep when he'd left the cockpit mid-flight, and he'd surprised himself by pausing to study her. He hadn't seen her on the countless Chicago to San Francisco flights he'd commanded in the last few years.

"Joining us for dinner, Mike?"

He reluctantly shifted his gaze from the brunette to the blonde staring at him hopefully.

Shaking his head, he gave her a closemouthed smile. "Not tonight. I've got some paperwork to catch-up on before I'm out of here."

"I'll wait for you, have a drink until you're done."

Mike sensed the innuendo in the voice of the woman almost young enough to be his daughter. He had a strict no mixing business with pleasure policy. And Caitlin would definitely be pleasure. "You guys go on," he told her. "Maybe next time."

"All right." He felt Caitlin's eyes trail his to the only remaining passenger in the first-class cabin. "You have my cell in case you change your mind." She stepped aside, allowing the cleaning crew to enter before lifting the handle of her wheeled bag. "Good night."

"Good night," Mike threw over his shoulder. The woman had flawless olive skin and her lips shimmered with the same shade of pink gloss that glazed her fingernails. Holding the phone in the crook of her shoulder, she was writing furiously on an envelope. He looked on as she disconnected, then slipped the phone into her enormous purse and stood. Mike nearly tripped over his feet trying to reach her before she slid her carry-on out of the overhead compartment.

"Let me get that." Reaching over her head, he grabbed the bag. It was heavier than he expected. "Long trip?"

"Just a week or so," she answered with a bright smile. "I've been through the lost luggage nightmare twice. I've learned to carry all the essentials with me."

She was so naturally, effortlessly beautiful, Mike couldn't imagine she needed much. "I hope our airline didn't lose your luggage," he remarked.

"No." Her silky hair rested just below her shoulders and her eyes paralleled its dark hue. "Neither time," she hastened to inform him.

"Good to hear."

Their gaze held for a moment more. Then she broke it by saying, "Thank you." She started to reach for the bag.

"This is awfully heavy. I'll carry it out for you."

"That's not necessary. I can get it."

"I insist." Mike extended his arm, gesturing for her to walk ahead of him.

She obliged, walking toward the exit on excruciatingly long legs. She stopped at the breezeway and started to say something, but the roar of the vacuums foiled it. She followed his silent direction and when they reached the gate said, "Thanks."

"My pleasure." Mike found himself oddly compelled to make conversation. "Is San Francisco your final destination?" He was torn between not wanting to let her go and not wanting her to miss a connection.

"Yes, I'm in town for a wedding. I also have some business meetings planned for next week. I don't get out to the West Coast very often anymore."

"Anymore?"

"I went to school out here." She sent an expectant glance down to the bag Mike was still holding. "Thank you again, Captain."

He wanted to ask her where, but her tone had become businesslike and he sensed she was ready to be on her way. "Of course. And it's Mike. Mike Savoy." He set the bag at her feet. She smelled as good as she looked.

"Delaney Richards." She extended her hand. "It's nice to meet you, Mike."

"Likewise." Her hand felt as silky smooth as her hair looked. He found himself wanting run his hands through it just to make sure. "Where are you staying?"

The random question seemed to surprise her as much as it had him. "The Fairmont," she informed him.

"Along with being beautiful, you have excellent taste. You can't go wrong there."

"So I've heard." She blushed a little. "Well, I should get to baggage claim before my suitcase goes to lost and found."

Mike laughed without opening his mouth. "You are a seasoned traveler, Ms. Richards."

"Delaney. And yes, I am. The East Coast and Europe for the most part."

"I've traveled the world myself. But there's no place quite like San Francisco." He handed her the bag. "Enjoy your stay."

"I will."

He watched her disappear into the sea of people. He'd never taken such interest in a passenger before. Not that she seemed to mind. She was traveling alone and not wearing an engagement or wedding ring. Maybe he would see her again on her outbound flight. Or better yet in the city. After all, the Fairmont was only a few blocks from his apartment on Nob Hill.

❦

It was after midnight Chicago time when Delaney arrived in her room. But thanks to her cross-country nap, she wouldn't be going to sleep anytime soon. Gazing at the lights meandering up and down Telegraph Hill, she was reminded of how much she loved San Francisco. The clanking of cable cars and bellowing of foghorns brought her back to the days before impossible deadlines, endless meetings and most of all, a broken heart. Of all the things she'd imagined going wrong on her wedding day, finding herself alone at the altar hadn't made the list.

And she hadn't been anywhere near a wedding since.

There'd been plenty of invitations in the last two years, of course. All of which she'd found a convenient reason to decline. But this one was different. This was Lindsay.

They'd gone from randomly assigned roommates to fast friends in college. Lindsay and Delaney instantly bonded over a myriad of commonalities. Most notably not having a father in their lives, albeit for completely different reasons. Lindsay had lost her parents as a child; Delaney had never known her father. Which made it all the more peculiar that he'd had been coming to mind so much lately. She was pushing down the past again when Lindsay's ring tone interrupted her thoughts.

"Welcome back to California." The joy in her friend's voice was palpable.

"Thanks. It's good to be back. How's the bride?"

"Better now that the winds have calmed. The smoke from the brush fires in the foothills made its way up here. Keep your fingers crossed that Saturday will be clear."

"Either way everything will be beautiful," Delaney reassured her.

There was dead air for a long moment, then Lindsay said, "It means so much to me that you came, Laney."

Delaney felt her eyes well with tears. But at least her stomach didn't clench anymore. Or threaten to empty. "I wouldn't miss it for the world," she told her and meant it.

"Can you drive up first thing? That way we can catch-up before everything gets crazy tomorrow night."

"Sure." Delaney assessed her reflection in the full-length mirror with a self-deprecating grimace. "I could use a little Tahoe sun."

"That can be arranged. I was afraid you'd be delayed. Fog shut down SFO for a few hours. You were lucky to have gotten in on time."

She felt a smile sneak in and reverse the crescent moon-like frown on her mouth. "Yeah, today must be my lucky day."

CHAPTER TWO

THE MORNING SUNLIGHT STREAMING through Mike's bedroom window woke him despite the pillow covering his head. He'd been in the air more than not these last few weeks and had been looking forward to some sleep. So much for that. He grabbed a sweatshirt and went to the kitchen to make coffee. While it brewed, he leafed through a week's worth of mail, assessing what needed to be addressed before the weekend with a operose sigh. This last rotation had been a decidedly long haul. Steaming mug in hand, he scooped up the pertinent mail and went outside. Both sets of French doors opened onto a small deck and today Mike chose the one facing east. He sank into the deck chair as the caws of seagulls and the hum of traffic filled the air. Resting his gaze on the Fairmont, he wondered what Delaney Richards was doing this fine morning.

She'd mentioned being in town for a wedding, presumably this weekend, but didn't say how long into next week she'd be staying. Or whom she'd be staying with, he reminded himself with a grunt. Surely such a beautiful woman wouldn't be at loose ends at a wedding. He was still mulling that over when Bruce Springsteen's gravelly voice filled the air.

"Mr. Savoy?"

"Speaking."

"This is the Hyatt Hotel and Casino Lake Tahoe, calling to confirm your Presidential Suite reservation for tonight."

"That's right." Mike consulted his watch. "I should be there around five o'clock. You have my credit card number for the deposit."

"Yes, that's all been taken care of. I understand this is a bachelor party. There is nothing to indicate that refreshments," the caller cleared his throat as if speaking in code, "or anything else is scheduled to be delivered to the room. Are you planning to enjoy the gaming and restaurants on the property? Or can we bring everything to you, perhaps?"

Chuckling, Mike put the man out of his misery. "That won't be necessary." He was long over that kind of bachelor party as was the groom. "There will only be a few of us. The rehearsal dinner is being held on the property as well, at Hues of Blue. We'll be doing some gambling afterwards. There's no live entertainment, per se."

There was a relieved sigh on the other end of the line. "Very good then. We'll look forward to seeing you this afternoon and accommodating you for the next few days."

Mike responded in kind, then reverted his eyes to the Fairmont. He would probably be too busy over the weekend to give Delaney Richards a second thought. But just in case, he'd better decide where to ask her to dinner when he got back.

Watson Brewer had done his due diligence, but a picture was worth a thousand words. And he didn't want to head up to Folsom until he had something concrete. His plan had been to hop on a plane to Chicago, kill two birds with one stone. But the old lady alone wasn't worth the trek. It was the girl. For a guy who hadn't seen his kid in two decades, Colton Richards sure yapped about her a lot, he snickered to himself. He nodded to the man in the red suit trimmed in gold and opted for the revolving door. The lobby lived up to its reputation, but didn't compare to the Bellagio or the Venetian by a long shot.

"Welcome to the Fairmont. Checking in, sir?"

Watson flashed his best smile. "Just visiting a guest. Delaney Richards. I've forgotten the room number."

"It's against hotel policy to give out room numbers, but I can confirm if the guest is registered. You can use the house phone to contact her." The woman half his age punched at the keyboard on the opposite side of the massive oak desk. Then her smile gave way to a frown. "I'm sorry. Ms. Richards checked out this morning."

Watson swore under his breath, but kept his calculated smile bright. "I'm sure she said she'd be in town through the weekend."

"Perhaps she had a last minute change of plans."

Not according to his source at the airline. He ground his teeth, but didn't let the frustration color his voice. "How odd that she wouldn't have mentioned it. Could there be another reservation?"

The clerk narrowed her eyes in suspicion. "That information is confidential. But if you leave your card, I can pass it along should Ms. Richards return."

"That won't be necessary. I'll find another way to contact her," he replied smoothly. "Thanks for checking." He turned on his heel and retraced his steps, feeling her skeptical stare on his back. Stepping out into the midmorning sunshine, he reached into his jacket pocket and pulled out the photograph. She sure was pretty. Pretty enough to be noticed. He shifted his gaze to the doorman, helping an elderly woman out of a taxi. He'd hoped to fly in a little lower on the radar than that. Questions raise more questions, he reminded himself. And he wanted to be the only asking them.

❧

Lake Tahoe sparkled like diamonds under the boundless blue sky as Delaney entered Incline Village. The estate-like homes shrouded by towering pine trees were as large as the apartment building she'd grown up in, she reminded herself in awe. Reaching her destination, she threw the rental SUV into park and took a couple of deep breaths. She was giving herself props for making it this far when a tap on the window startled her. The eyes looking back at her were as cobalt a blue as the lake itself and the grin as wide as its breadth. Delaney felt the butterflies in her stomach start to settle as she opened the door and stood. Lindsay took her into a warm embrace and hugged her so tight that the two women rocked in place.

"Let me look at you," Lindsay said by way of greeting, giving Delaney a thorough once-over. "Gorgeous as ever, but a little too thin."

"You sound like my mother. I do eat."

With a skeptical squint, she dropped an arm around Delaney's shoulders and led her up the flagstone paved path. "We'll have to work on that this weekend. I can't wait to catch-up. We'll get your bag later."

They reached the two-tiered deck lined with red and white impatiens. "The blue will have to be sky," Lindsay said, reading Delaney's mind. "Note to self, it's impossible to find blue annuals."

"You did all of this yourself?" She took in the perfectly manicured yard, bursting with plants and flowers of all sizes and colors. "When you said you were gardening, I figured you meant a few pots."

"I had to channel my nervous energy somehow. It became a labor of love." Lindsay gestured to one of the chairs circling a slate top table. "Sit. I'll get us something to drink."

"I've been sitting for four hours," Delaney countered, walking to the edge of the deck and imbibing the fresh mountain air. "I'll be right here."

"Suit yourself," Lindsay tossed over her shoulder, blonde ponytail swinging like a pendulum on the back of her head.

Feeling more relaxed than she had in recent memory, Delaney contemplated the water lapping the fawn-colored shore. Her gaze was shifting upward, where rows of pines and aspens dotted the Sierras like soldiers standing at attention when Lindsay returned.

"Amazing how it looks the same, isn't?" Standing next to her, Lindsay handed Delaney a glass of iced tea. "No matter how long you've been away."

"It's magnificent." Delaney took a sip. "A sight for sore eyes from high-rises and strip malls."

"You have a lake in Chicago too, if I remember correctly," Lindsay pointed out with humor shining in her eyes.

"Not like this. I feel like I'm in another world. The air is so crisp, so clean."

"Speaking of clean." Shooting Delaney an pointed stare over the rim of her glass, Lindsay said, "Time for you to."

Delaney played dumb. "Time for me to what?"

"To come clean. You're still not yourself. I could hear it in your voice every time we spoke. What's going on?"

"Nothing's going on," Delaney shot back inadequately.

"Maybe that's the problem. Have you had a night out lately?"

"I'm going to have one tonight, aren't I? And tomorrow night as well."

"I mean a night out with a man." Delaney opened her mouth to speak, but Lindsay barreled over her. "Not business-related. How long has it been?"

"I don't know." Delaney's glance momentarily escaped to the sanctity of the rustic, craftsman-style house. "Is Brian around? I'm dying to meet him."

"He's in Reno picking up his daughter at the airport. Stop trying to change the subject."

Lindsay's eyes softened as she went on. "It hurts me to see you like this, letting your life go by. If Ryan walked in here right now, would you forgive him and take him back?"

"No, of course not," Delaney said and meant it.

"Then what are you waiting for? How many dates have you turned down?"

Delaney took a tasteless sip of tea. "None."

"None?" Lindsay amazed. "Are all the men in Chicago blind? Or married?"

"Hardly," Delaney began with a grunt. "I don't really have the time or desire to date. Didn't you feel that way too?"

Lindsay looked away as if mentally rewinding time, then replied heedfully, "Yes, Brian and I both felt that way. That's the difference. Ryan has gone on with his life. You need to do the same." She hesitated, then placing both glasses on the top of the deck railing, took Delaney's hands in hers. "He's not coming back for you, Laney."

"I know." Delaney fixed her eyes on the brown ski runs breaking up the verdant hills. "I realized that even before he eloped." She heaved a sigh. "I don't want him to. I guess somewhere along the way I gave up on true love."

"I did too. So much so that I almost married Paul." She turned Delaney by the shoulders to face her and looked her square in the eye. "I understand what it feels like to love someone that much and lose them. But what you had with Ryan wasn't true love. So your true love is out there somewhere, waiting for you."

❧

Mike pushed the elevator call button repeatedly, frustrated with himself for getting a late start. Lindsay would be frantic by the time he got to the restaurant. Normally he would revel in getting under her skin, but this was different. As was going to a wedding without a date. Even if he and Jessica hadn't called it quits, he wouldn't have asked her to fly in. There were several women he might have asked if the wedding had been in San Francisco, but this was a weekend, not an evening. Too complicated.

Being in Tahoe again, however, was not complicated. Much of his childhood had been spent here, swimming in the lake in the summer and skiing through forests of frost-painted trees in the winter. He'd been thinking about diversifying his investments and buying a place up here would definitely complement his portfolio.

He walked briskly through the lobby, making mental notes of the casino's layout for later. The last fringes of daylight were sliding behind the milky-white peaks of the Sierra Nevadas as he made his way through the lakeside restaurant. He put on an apologetic frown and clasped Brian's shoulders from behind. "Sorry I'm late."

Brian rose and took Mike into a brotherly hug. "No problem. We're just getting started."

"Hi, Uncle Mike," came a soft voice from the table.

Mike bent down and kissed Brian's daughter on the cheek. "Hi, yourself. How's the most beautiful sophomore at USC?"

"I don't know. I'm a technically a junior after the summer session."

"That's impossible. Just last week you were playing Barbies in my living room," he teased. Secretly, that gave Mike pause. Kelsey had grown into a beautiful girl, the splitting image of her mother, with sable hair to Brian's blonde and hazel eyes to his blue.

Brian shifted his proud gaze to the rest of the table. "Mike, you remember Moira Brody."

"Of course." Mike extended his hand to the fair-faced woman with a headful of black ringlet curls. "Nice to see you again."

Instead of shaking it, she jumped up and embraced Mike from across the table. "You too," she replied, emerald eyes sparkling.

The man beside her stood and offered his hand. "Paul Webster. Nice to meet you."

Mike responded in kind and a silent message passed between them. Then his eyes swept the table draped in white linen and glistening china. "Where's Lindsay?"

"Ladies room. She was getting a little restless waiting for the best man," Brian told him with a chuckle in his eyes. "If you don't want wine, go order a beer. My tab is open."

Nodding in affirmation, Mike headed over to the mahogany bar. Brian had the best table in the house tonight, directly in front of the ceiling-to-floor window wall. When Mike looked beyond it, he saw a fire pit surrounded by Adirondack chairs and wooden benches. He was debating how far the deck extended onto the beach when he heard a familiar voice call his name. But when Mike turned around, he found the last person he could have expected. He felt his jaw drop, then blinked hard a few times, assuming she would disappear or morph into someone else.

But she didn't.

Then he realized Lindsay was hugging him. "You made it," she said. "I was getting a little nervous." She broke away and gestured to the woman at her side. "Mike, this is—"

"Delaney Richards," he managed to finish for her.

Lindsay's gaze sliced between them in awe. "You two know each other?"

"I brought her plane in last night."

"And carried my bag out to the gate for me," Delaney added.

"This is the wedding you flew in for?"

A warm smile replaced the astonishment in her eyes. "Lindsay was my roommate in college."

"Brian is my next door neighbor."

"You're the best man?"

Mike could do nothing but nod.

They were still beholding each other when Lindsay cleared her throat and interjected, "Well, I'd better get back to the table." She directed her parting words at Delaney. "I'll meet you there. Take your time."

Delaney's lips parted slightly and she watched Lindsay walk away, as if unsure whether to follow. Not wanting her to, Mike instantly stepped forward. "Can I get you a drink?" She smelled intoxicating; spicy and sexy, akin to the strapless dress she wore.

"No thanks," she declined, meeting his gaze again. "I have a glass of wine at the table."

Mike simply could not take his eyes off of her. After a long moment, Delaney suggested, "We should probably get back there too."

Mike grabbed his beer from the bar and extended his arm. "After you."

She complied, seemingly unaware of the male heads turning to undress her with their eyes as she walked toward the table. Of which Mike was one.

She turned, as if sensing he wasn't behind her, and cocked her head to the side with a puzzled expression. "Mike? Are you coming?"

Mike shook off the stupor and made quick work of the space between them. Then, placing his hand at the small of her back without touching her, he guided her across the room.

There were still three vacant chairs at the table, one with a bird's-eye view of the water and the mountains and two on the opposite side, facing the restaurant. Delaney stopped in front of one of the latter and addressed Kelsey, "Am I losing it, or did you move?"

Before Kelsey could respond, Lindsay piped up. "I asked her to scoot over so we could chat. You don't mind, do you?"

"Of course not." Delaney replied, starting to pull out one of the chairs.

Mike beat her to it. "Here," he offered hurriedly as their arms brushed. He wondered if she'd also felt the dizzying twinge.

"Thanks." She tossed him a look from under her lashes and sat down. And without a second's debate Mike took the chair next to her, opting for the better view.

CHAPTER THREE

"WHAT WERE YOU AND Mike talking about all evening?" Lindsay asked a few hours later as she, Moira and Delaney sat on the deck drinking wine.

"This and that," Delaney answered dreamily. "Chicago for one thing. He's familiar with it from layovers. And neither one of us could get over the coincidence of seeing each other again."

"So you remembered him right away too?"

Delaney affirmed with a nod. "I thought I was hallucinating at first."

"How could you not remember Mike?" Moira chimed in. "With those gorgeous eyes and that disarming smile."

"I know," Lindsay agreed. "Brian says Mike is the most eligible bachelor on Nob Hill."

"And he's smart," Moira added. "You have to be, to make captain so young. He's never been married, right, Linds?"

"No. And the entire time I've known him he hasn't even dated anyone seriously."

"He must be waiting for just the right one," Moira suggested conspiratorially. "Is he bringing anyone to the wedding?"

"Unbelievably no."

Delaney was starting to catch on. She sent them each a discerning look. "Okay you guys, I get the message." Secretly, she was glowing inside. Mike seemed to have enjoyed the evening as much as she had. But so had Ryan, she reminded herself, feeling the glow fade. Three years worth of evenings. But a lifetime, not so much.

"I don't know what you mean," Lindsay connived.

Moira returned Lindsay's wink and held her glass up in the air. "A toast. To the most eligible bachelor on Nob Hill. And the unsuspecting passenger who caught his eye."

Lindsay touched her glass to Moira's. "I'll drink to that."

Reminding herself tonight wasn't about her, Delaney joined her glass with theirs. "And to the best friend a girl could have." She consulted her watch. It was just past midnight. "On the best day of her life. To Lindsay and—"

"Brian?" Lindsay astonished under her breath, squinting over Delaney's shoulder. By the time she turned around, Lindsay was running to greet him. He gathered her in his arms and whispered something indistinguishable in her ear before taking her mouth in a telling kiss.

"And to think they almost didn't make it," Moira said with a catch in her voice.

Delaney bit back her own wistfulness. "From what I hear, you had a lot to do with making sure they did."

"Maybe a little. The rest was fate." She clinked her glass against Delaney's. "To the fates. For bringing Lindsay and Brian together again." She cocked her head and continued with a furtive smile. "Your work here is not yet done."

After what appeared to be a few minutes of coaxing and negotiation, mostly on Brian's part, Lindsay and Brian came over to say good night. After they exchanged parting pleasantries, Moira topped off both her and Delaney's glasses, killing the bottle.

"Speaking of fate, you and Paul looked awfully cozy tonight," Delaney pointed out.

"We're taking it slow. It's still a little weird."

Delaney imagined so. "Not as weird as Lindsay and Paul almost getting married. How did all that come about? And so fast?"

Moira began with care. "Between her grandmother's death and the split with Brian, Lindsay was vulnerable, scared, alone. Paul was there to pick up the pieces and one thing led to another."

"Until?"

"Until Lindsay had an epiphany of sorts. She finally listened to her heart. And that little voice inside her head. "

Delaney nodded in understanding. "How did you and Paul end up together?"

Moira's smile trembled a little. "We've all been friends forever. Then one day it changed for me. Of course he was perpetually in love with Lindsay. I figured my infatuation would pass."

Delaney, impressed by Moira's candor, prompted, "But it didn't."

Moira shook her head from side to side saying, "No matter how hard I tried. After forcing herself to be honest and call off the wedding, Lindsay moved on to me. Then she started playing matchmaker, all the way from San Francisco." Her eyes danced with goodwill and humor. "She's good at that, just so you know."

"Yeah," Delaney agreed, pointing over Moira's shoulder. "She sure is."

Eyes filling with confusion, Moira turned her head, then stood slowly. "Hey." Her tone took a nuanced turn upward. "What are you doing here?"

Paul was approaching them with a hopeful smile. "Listening to the darkness," he answered, brushing his lips across Moira's. "Hi."

She greeted him in kind. "How'd everything go?"

"Awful. We all lost our shirts."

"I mean with Brian," she clarified.

"Fine. Now that we've buried the hatchet, I kind of like him."

"He said the same thing about you." Then she shifted her gaze to Delaney and rolled her eyes. "Men are so different. They slug it out once and it's over. No grudges."

"Is Brian here?" Paul looked into the kitchen, lit up like a Christmas tree. "He didn't head toward the elevators either."

"You just missed him," Moira informed him. "He whisked Lindsay away a few minutes ago."

"So much for the old adage about bad luck."

"According to Brian, there is no such thing. Every couple sleeps together on their wedding day. Whether it's before or after the ceremony is immaterial."

"Lindsay fell for it, huh?"

"I didn't even try to talk her out of it."

"And you?" Paul addressed Delaney.

"With my track record, who am I to argue?" she told him with odd levity, then heard herself say, "But I'm getting over it. It's taken a long time, but I think I'm actually getting over it."

❧

Curious to see what was for sale in the area, Mike decided to take a walk on the beach. Or so he told himself. The moonbeams flirted with the inky water as he slowed his pace, looking on as the ripples dissipated and the water became placid again. Then came another pebble. He stood in the coarse sand, adjusting his eyes to the darkness and honing in on the figure at the shore. Until, as if suddenly clairvoyant, her shoulders squared and tightened. She stood and whirled around, the city girl in her ready to run.

"Delaney? It's Mike."

She squinted in the murky light, as if mentally matching his voice with his face. Then with a stabilizing breath, brought a hand to her heart. "Oh! You scared me for a second."

"Sorry." He began walking toward her. "What are you doing out here?"

"Too wired to sleep." She met him halfway. "And it's just so beautiful."

She certainly was. He swallowed hard. "Where are Lindsay and Moira?"

"They each got a better offer," she told him easily. "Brian couldn't live without Lindsay for even one night. Paul showed up not long after that. He and Moira went for," she made air quotes with her fingers, "a walk. I didn't want to hold them back."

Mike wanted to hold *her*. "Bastards. They were probably losing on purpose. I knew Brian wasn't playing to his card sense."

"Brian, maybe. Paul, no. He's not that disingenuous. He's just beginning to realize that he's a little bit in love with Moira. It's sweet."

He might not be the only one, Mike shocked himself by thinking. "That's awfully deep for this hour."

"Must be the wine. Oh, my glass is still down there." She turned back toward the shore. He fell into step beside her. "How about you? What are you doing out so late?"

Mike shrugged. "Just felt like going for a walk." And finding you...

"Too much bachelor party, huh?"

"Bachelor party is a pretty loose term. We hit the blackjack tables and had a few beers." Reaching the shore, Mike retrieved the glass and handed it to Delaney. Their fingers brushed, but unlike earlier, his stomach didn't jump and settle. It tugged. Hard. "Here you go."

"Thanks." She cleared her throat nervously as if she'd felt it too. "You know, the ceremony is going to be right here. It'll be lovely at sunset."

"It's lovely now," Mike told her. He hadn't noticed the flecks of gold in her coffee-colored eyes before. Because he'd never been this close to her before. "Even the alpenglow doesn't compare to you in the moonlight." He took a step closer, closing the small space between them. She was suddenly as still as a statue, holding his eyes in hers. Dropping his gaze to her mouth, he rested a hand on each side of her face and brought her to him.

Her eyelids went to half-mast as his lips hovered over hers in anticipation. If not for the want growing inside him, he would have kept them there longer, taking in all of her properly. But her scent was filling the small cavity between them, driving him forward. Their mouths were close enough now that he could taste the sweet summer night on her breath, mingling with the red wine and the chocolate cake served for dessert. Gently, he laid his lips on hers. Slowly at first, he began to move his mouth over them, sampling. He wanted to inhale her little by little, fill every part of him with her touch, her taste, her presence, bit by bit. But her mouth was like a lodestone, latching on to his. He had to have more of her, had to dive deeper, had to go faster to meet the insatiable need rising inside him. He had to have her whole mouth.

She met him head-on and reciprocated. She was incredibly responsive, exceedingly generous. The pull in his stomach shot upward, sending his heart cantering and his chest swelling as the waves crashed incessantly against the shore at their feet. Their tongues flirted, skirted, melded until not a shared breath remained between them. Then Mike buried his face in her hair and through strangled breaths admitted, "I've been wanting to do that since I first laid eyes on you last night."

She seemed as winded as he but managed, "I've wanted you to."

He tore himself away, stealing a kiss on the way. "I still can't believe you're here. I was thinking about you."

The inkling of a smile curved the corners of her mouth and mixed with the need and uneasiness in her eyes. "I was thinking about you too."

Shelving the desire to kiss her again, he tucked her hand in his and led her slowly up the beach toward the house. "You must be exhausted. It's four a.m. your time."

"I'm on adrenaline, I guess."

So was he. From that kiss. From her.

"I need to go to bed, though. Tomorrow will be another late night."

"You're going to be here tomorrow, right? I didn't imagine this?"

She laughed a little. "For one thing, tomorrow is today. And if you imagined it, so did I."

"Let me do this again, to make sure." Stopping, he captured her mouth, more greedily this time, nibbling on her top lip as he pulled away. "Yep. That was definitely real for me," he told her, wondering if the inner rush was noticeable. And mutual.

"Me too." Her tone was sincere, but her eyes were full of fear.

Mike made a mental note to ask Lindsay if there was a man in Delaney's life. He weighed the odds then said, "Delaney, I want to see you tomorrow."

"Since you're the best man and I'm sitting in the first row, I can guarantee it," she replied around a giggle.

"Will you be sitting with someone in the first row?"

Her eyes softened with understanding and she whispered, "No."

Feeling like he'd won the lottery, Mike rested his forehead on hers. "You are now."

CHAPTER FOUR

COLTON RICHARDS STARED AT the photograph in awe as if he'd never seen it before. But he knew every inch of the headshot from *Crain's Chicago Business*. He'd been an eighteen-year-old hot mess when she was born. Probably would have run right then if her mother's old man hadn't been such a dick. Threatened within an inch of his life, he'd made an honest woman out of her. He'd even worked two jobs to support her and the baby. But that got old real fast.

He'd been going crazy, loading trucks all day, delivering pizzas at night. He'd wanted to see the world, go to college, get the hell out of there.

So one day he did.

And that was the worst decision he'd ever made. And now after a quarter-century of wrongs, he was determined to do right. He'd stayed out of trouble this time around. No small feat because this stretch had been a big ask. But it would be his last.

He'd gone through the scenario a million times in his head. What he'd say, how he'd explain, how he'd beg her to forgive him. He'd been young, stupid, selfish. Her mother had been way out of his league. He would never have been good enough for either one of them.

But everything was different now. He'd earned a degree, become well-read and well-spoken. All in an attempt to prove he'd changed. That he was worthy of her. But that wasn't his first order of business. First he had to right another wrong.

"Richards!" The pimple-faced C.O. shouted.

The ill-fitting dress outs settled on his hips as Colton rose from wobbly plastic chair and approached the glass. "Yeah."

"You know the drill."

Colton signed the paper and sliding it under the window, exchanged it for a a shoe box-sized plastic box.

"The shuttle driver will distribute the bus tickets and gate money at the station. Good luck to you."

One debt down, two to go.

∽

"Care to dance?"

Delaney had been so fixated on Lindsay and Brian that she hadn't heard Mike come up from behind. She turned to him and wondered if the jump in her stomach was evident on her face. "I'd love to."

"You look absolutely stunning," he complimented, leading her out to the dance floor and taking her into his arms. "I kept catching myself staring at you. Almost missed my cue to give Brian the ring."

That ineffable feeling, a mixture of joy and desire tinged with apprehension, began surging inside of her again. She'd had a dreamless night's sleep and woke feeling rested for the first time in forever. They'd started the morning with mimosas and massages, and then joined by Kelsey, moved on to all manner of beautifying from head to toe. Delaney felt like she was walking on air. Looping Mike's neck with her arms, she lifted her eyes to his. "You look quite handsome yourself. And your speech was lovely."

"The speech was the easy part." He nodded toward the bride and groom. "Look at them."

He was right. And Delaney would have been just as googly-eyed on her wedding day. But the eyes looking back at her would have been lying.

"I was afraid I'd drop the ring in the sand," Mike was saying. "Can you see Brian and me digging for it? In suits and ties, no less."

"We could've borrowed a metal detector from the woman down the street. She's out on the beach every morning. You'd never know she's worth millions."

"Even better," Mike said around a chuckle. "Brian Rembrandt, Esquire, mining for gold in the sand."

The song ended, but they stood there for a few silent clicks, mouths only inches apart, eyes clinging, as if they were the only ones in the room. Finally Mike let out a shallow breath and said,

"Lindsay's throwing the bouquet. Do you want to go out there?"

Delaney shook off the reverie and shifted her gaze to the center of the dance floor. "Yeah, I guess I should. Thanks for the dance." She started to walk away, but he caught her hand and drew her back to him.

"Come right back. I'll wait here for you."

She gave him an affirming nod, then joined the circle of women gathered around Lindsay.

After a forewarning drumroll, the bride scanned the crowd, momentarily resting her gaze on Delaney. Then she turned around and flung the bouquet over her shoulder.

Directly into Delaney's hands.

Looking beyond pleased with herself, Lindsay rushed over as the guests clapped and cheered. "You caught it! I'm so glad it was you!"

Breaking out of Lindsay's embrace, Delaney looked up to find Mike' s eyes locked on her. He gave her a closemouthed smile and a thumbs up. The next thing she knew, the photographer arrived. "Nice catch," he praised from behind his lens. "Scoot a little closer, ladies. Big smiles." The two women obliged as the disc jockey's voice bellowed in the background. "Okay all you single guys out there. Now it's your turn."

"I guess that's my cue," Lindsay said, heading over to the chair in the middle of the dance floor. Delaney looked on as several men sauntered over and formed a circle. Mike was not one of them. Finally she spotted him at the bar with Brian. After a short debate, he hung his head defeatedly and followed the groom.

Delaney trailed them inertly. "She's Got Legs" blasted through the night air as Brian squatted in front of his wife and slid the lace garter down her leg with his teeth. Then, sporting a taunting grin, he twirled it on his forefinger and threw it directly at Mike. But it veered to the left and into the hands of another man. He looked like a quintessential California boy who had just stepped off his surfboard to attend the wedding. Mike shrugged good-naturedly and started walking toward her as the crowd dispersed and slow dance music began to play.

Just then Delaney heard a husky voice over her shoulder. "Ready?"

She found the voice's enthusiastic gaze. "Pardon?"

Displaying his catch proudly, the bronzed man explained, "To dance. It's tradition for the bouquet and garter recipients to dance together." He extended his hand. "I'm David Cummings."

She shook it. "Delaney Richards."

"Nice to meet you. Shall we?"

It was her obligation, she supposed. She scanned the room for Mike and came up empty. "Of course."

Taking her in his arms, he gave her a solid once-over and asked, "How do you know the bride and groom?"

Delaney gave him a perfunctory smile. "Lindsay was my roommate in college," she answered, wondering when David would find a home for his hands. "How about you?"

"Brian is a partner at my grandfather's firm. I'm doing an internship there this summer. To see if I want to go into law like the rest of the family."

"And?"

"It's fine." He shrugged indifferently. "I'm not sure if I've got the stones for law school, though."

The John Legend song played on and she heard David talking to her. But she was too busy looking for Mike to follow what he was saying.

Then his strong, confident voice came from behind. "May I?"

Delaney turned to see Mike sending David a loaded stare. Then irritated, but well-bred, David thanked her for the dance and stepped aside.

She watched his retreating back for a few seconds, then turned back to Mike. He gathered her into his arms. "I see you made a new friend."

Her arms wreathed his neck. "Yes, David I think it was." Her tone was deliberately coy.

"He didn't seem too happy about my cutting in. He's been staring at you all evening," Mike let her know, tightening his arm around her waist.

"Really? I hadn't noticed." But she had noticed how much she loved being in Mike's arms.

"I did. I didn't like it."

Her breath caught. "You didn't?"

"No. I also didn't like his hands all over you."

"That I did notice. I tried to keep them at bay."

His jaw tensed up. "I hope you didn't mind my cutting in."

How could he think she did? Because he couldn't feel the butterflies in her stomach, the way her heart was chasing them. She shook her head. "I was looking for you. I didn't know where you went."

"Sorry. Moira and I had to witness the marriage certificate."

"I only danced with...David because he caught the garter. It's tradition. Or so he says."

Mike nodded agreeably, like that made sense, and his eyes softened a little. "I guess I should have moved a little faster." He brought her body to his, the palm of his hand pressed to her bare back. Then, mouth hovering over hers, he whispered, "I thought I had it."

Delaney felt like her chest would burst if he didn't kiss her. "You do."

Their lips meet briefly, more gently, this time. Mike left her mouth to nuzzle her neck, just below the earlobe. She quivered a little inside and she wondered if he noticed. By the time his gaze returned to hers, the music had stopped and the dance floor had all but cleared. And the long forgotten desire spreading through Delaney's body had settled into the triangle between her thighs.

He skimmed her forehead with his lips. "Why is it that every time I want to kiss you there are about a hundred people around?"

"Are there?" She'd been so caught up in him, she'd forgotten her place.

"Let's get a drink. Go out on the beach."

At that moment Delaney would have gone anywhere with him. "Okay."

His hand slid into hers as they headed for the bar, then took the wide wooden steps down to the shore. "Want to walk down to the pier? They've renovated this property since the last time I was here. I'd like to check it out."

"Sure." Delaney debated a moment, then added, "Hold on." She slipped off her shoes and hung them from their entwined fingers.

They walked through the cool sand in silence for a few minutes, the silver stilettos swinging between them. Then Mike said, "Delaney, I have a confession to make."

Delaney's stomach sank but she kept her eyes fixed on the gently crashing waves approaching the shore. She knew he was too good to be true. He was probably seeing someone Lindsay didn't know about. He hadn't meant to start something with her, it had just happened. Now he had to let her down easy. At least the wedding was over. She'd never have to see him again after tonight.

Mike waved an impatient hand in front of her face. "Don't you want to know what it is?"

"I guess so," she replied, trying to sound indifferent.

He stopped and set his beer bottle down on a boulder under a cluster of pine trees. "I don't want to check out the pier."

"You don't?"

"No." Mike took the wine glass from her and set it next to the bottle, then cradled her face in his hands. "I want to be alone with you. I want to do this." He laid his lips on hers, tentatively at first, exploring, nibbling, waiting for her permission to take more. She returned the need, the rising passion, and surrendered to it. He latched his lips onto hers, nudging her mouth open with his and inching his tongue inside. She welcomed him, felt his building desire and answered it with her own, found herself drowning in it. He left her mouth on saw-offed breaths, and began kissing his way down her throat as their chests heaved against each other and their hearts pounded in unison. His hands were on her breasts now and her nipples were growing hard under his busy thumbs. She was pressed so tightly against him that she could feel his fly following suit. Her heart was beating wildly in her stomach, temples, chest, chasing his into some kind of hedonic oblivion. Then he ripped his mouth away.

"Laney," he muttered, panting out of her embrace, he stepped back and glued the palms of his hands to his knees and shook his head from side to side. "I had to stop before it was too late. You have no idea how badly I want to take you back to my room." He scanned the beach restlessly. "Or improvise."

She did, actually. "Mike, we—"

Holding up his hand, he interrupted her. "I know. We can't. Not with those eyes."

⤴

She was deadpanning him, her sable eyes wide and breasts heaving in that low-cut black dress trimmed in rhinestones. He'd never seen that combination of desire and fear in someone's eyes before, especially those of a woman.

And he had to know why Delaney Richards had it in hers.

Because until he did, he wouldn't be making love to her. Clearly, she wanted him too; that wasn't the problem. The passion, albeit conflicted, was definitely there, threatening to overtake the apprehension. Or was that a reflection of his own?

Delaney cocooned herself, instantly frozen. He could almost see the wall going up around her, boxing her in. And him out. Straightening, he brought her back to him. "Laney, talk to me.

Lindsay said you weren't seeing anyone. So that's not it."

The panic in her eyes eased a little, as if his knowing that pleased her. She swallowed hard. "What else did she tell you?"

"She said you broke off an engagement a few years ago." Maybe that was it, the guy kept bothering her, stalking her. The mere thought of it made Mike's blood boil.

He watched as she broke away from him and walked to the shore. "I'll have to thank Lindsay for her discretion." She contemplated the lake for a long moment, then confirmed around a hollow laugh, "No, I'm not seeing anyone. There hasn't been anyone in my life since my fiancé." She turned around and looked at him through eyes full of pain. "And he broke off the engagement, not me." She stiffened, then finished. "On our wedding day."

Mike found that incomprehensible. "My God, Laney, I'm sorry. I don't know what to say."

"I think everything has already been said. Over and over again." She let out a determined breath. "And I'm finally getting over it too."

"Then why are you looking at me like a deer in headlights?" He went to her and stroked her cheek with the back of his hand. He wanted to draw her to him again, but thought better of it.

She gave him an tentative shrug. "I'm scared."

"Of me?"

"No," she decided out loud. "*Because* of you. For the first time I want to be over it."

He tipped her chin with his forefinger. "I'll take that as a tremendous compliment." With a soft kiss, he brushed away the strands of hair blowing across her face.

"I have a confession of my own to make," she stated, smiling up at him. "I was wondering if you were seeing someone too. Lindsay actually offered the information before I could ask."

Unbelievably pleased, he joined their hands. Hers were cold. And he wanted nothing more than to warm her. From the inside. Instead, he began walking. "I'm not. Not yet, anyway. But I met the most amazing woman and I want to get to know her better."

Her eyes grew damp with promise and she squeezed his hand.

He returned the encouragement, asking, "When are you going back to San Francisco?"

"Tuesday or Wednesday. You?"

"Monday." Unless I have a reason to stay, he silently added. "What are your plans tomorrow?"

"I don't have plans other than the brunch in the morning."

"I'll be there too. How about dinner?"

"I'd like that."

"What time is good for you?"

"Anytime is fine. I don't have any plans, remember?"

Mike stopped walking and brought her to him. "I remember. I just can't believe it. How can a woman like you not have plans every night?"

"For one thing, I haven't wanted to." She gulped. "Until now."

"So I guess I had it after all," he whispered, his lips loitering over hers.

Mumbling in agreement, she fell into his kiss.

CHAPTER FIVE

"BRIAN IS GOING TO kill you if you bring one more thing." Delaney lay on the bed in the master bedroom, head propped up on her elbows, and watched Lindsay pack.

"I know, I know," Lindsay conceded, assessing the ankle-length dress in the mirror. "But I bought this Hilo Hattie the first time we went to Maui. Brian has the matching shirt. God knows where it is, though." She threw it on the bed and grabbed another dress from the closet. "Or I could bring this one," she suggested, holding up a shorter version of the discarded one. "You'd never know it's from Old Navy."

"That one," advised Delaney. "It shows off your legs. Providing Brian lets you out of the room and you have somewhere to wear it."

"Very funny." But she deposited it in the suitcase. "Enough about me. Where are you and Mike going to dinner?"

"I don't know. He was going to ask Brian for a recommendation."

"You can't go wrong anywhere with a view this time of year. Even if the restaurant has an off night, it's worth it." She cleared her throat and began organizing her cosmetic bag. "Mike's going home tomorrow, right?"

"I think so."

"Did you tell him you were staying here for a few days?"

"Yeah."

Lindsay muttered something about her hair dryer and continued offhandedly, "I have an idea. Why don't you stay at our apartment in San Francisco instead of at the hotel?"

"That's not necessary, Linds. I have a healthy expense account."

"I know. But you'd have more room, be more comfortable there." She zipped her suitcase. "Kelsey hasn't been there lately, so her room is ready. It's up to you, of course."

Later Delaney would see through her friend's benevolent ruse. But for now, she played right into Lindsay's hands. "Okay, thanks. I could walk to the office from there."

"Then it's all settled," Lindsay triumphed. The oversized bag hit the wood floor with a thud. "Make yourself at home," she said as a door creaked open below. "I'll text you the alarm code and the particulars."

"Linds, we've got to go!" Brian's orotund voice came from downstairs along with the sound of approaching footfalls. "Tell me you're packed." Meeting the women on the landing, he grunted at Lindsay's bulging suitcase in mocked irritation. Then he picked it up and carried it out to the car.

"Thanks again for coming." Lindsay took Delaney into an affecting embrace. "It means so much to me."

"I know. Me, too." Delaney returned the hearty squeeze. "Because now I can see how incredibly happy you are."

Breaking away, Lindsay dabbed the corners of her eyes. "I am. And you will be too. In ways you never thought possible."

As Delaney watched them pull away, she almost believed that for the first time.

Almost, Delaney reminded herself a few hours later. She sat on the lower deck, listening to the waves pummel the shore. Mike had said six-thirty and it was after seven o'clock. There was probably a perfectly logical explanation for the delay. If something had come up, it was virtually impossible for Mike to reach her. They'd been in constant contact all weekend, giving them no reason to exchange numbers. Brian and Lindsay, the obvious remedy to that, were on a plane high above the Pacific. Delaney didn't dare call the hotel. All she could do was wait.

Her breath caught in her throat when a car whizzed around the corner. She huffed a snort when she realized it was wasn't a Porsche, but a Range Rover. And it was pulling into the driveway next door. She took a generous sip of wine, closing her eyes and exhaling deeply as the silky warmth slid down her throat. Thank God she hadn't slept with him. At least she knew that wasn't the reason for any disenchantment. She was a little out of practice.

The next time she glanced at her phone, another twenty minutes had gone by. Even if Mike showed, their reservation was no doubt lost. A convenient excuse to cancel the evening all together. Draining her glass, Delaney went inside to pour another. Luckily, Lindsay had an extensive wine collection in which she could drown her sorrows. She returned the unused glass to the cabinet with a shaking hand as tears began trickling down her cheeks. She'd felt an immediate connection with Mike and the feeling had appeared to be mutual. Choking back the past, she slammed the cabinet door, then shoved the cork back into the bottle with matching conviction. She was debating whether or not to take the bottle out to the deck to save herself a trip later when a rustling from behind had her spinning on her heel.

❧

Mike had been contemplating Delaney from the threshold of the deck door for a full thirty seconds. Hungrily. Her liquid silk mane skimmed her shoulders and he tried to push the thought of it spread out on pillow beneath him from his mind. Or those dancer's legs, hugged in denim tonight, wrapped around his in bed, especially if the rest of her was as voluptuous as the snug-fitting top she wore suggested. Convinced she got sexier every time he saw her, he put on a contrite smile and opened his mouth to speak. At the very second she whirled around. After a sharp intake of air, she stood frozen in place and studied him through wide eyes awash with despair and heartbreak. Then he realized what she must have thought.

That he wasn't coming.

He swallowed the apologetic words and approaching her unwaveringly, took her in his arms. He felt the whimpering in her chest before it became painfully audible. A long, heavy moment passed. Then he leaned his head back just enough to meet her eyes. They were brimming with tears. "I got caught behind an accident," he explained. "I had no way to get a hold of you. I'm so sorry."

She didn't reply at first, just caught her breath and tightened her grip around his middle. Even encased in his arms, she was trembling. "It's okay," she managed. "All that matters is that you're here now."

"Then why are you crying?" he asked, angling out of her embrace a step and drying her cheeks with his thumbs.

"Am I?" She dabbed the corners of her eyes in wonder.

"Yeah. A lot."

"It's just that..." Her voice trailed off, then she began again. "I'm so happy you're here. I thought maybe you changed your mind."

Wanting to strangle the ass who'd ruined her, Mike grabbed her by the upper arms. "How could I change my mind when you're the only thing on my mind? I was afraid you'd be angry," he admitted. "Instead you're heartbroken. And that's much worse." Inwardly surprised and ashamed at how much that pleased him, he brought her back against him. "I'm not going to do that to you. I'm not going to change my mind about tonight or anything else." He hesitated, then asked, "Are you?"

"Am I what?"

"Going to change your mind. About me." He left her and began to pace. For all he knew, she might not want to start a relationship with him. After all, they lived two thousand miles apart. And she obviously didn't trust him.

"I couldn't change my mind if I wanted to. That's what scares me. You're right; I was heartbroken at the prospect of you not coming."

He returned to her. "Well, I'm here now."

She considered him briefly before taking a restorative breath. "You sure are." She linked her arms around his neck and captured his mouth in hers. Mike felt his muscles go limp and the blood in his veins begin to pulsate—in one organ in particular. He'd been craving her mouth since the last time he'd had it. And after this he knew he'd be craving it again. Delaney taking the initiative only made him want her more.

He exhaled a cutting breath. "Laney, something is happening between us. We have to trust each other. Can you do that? Can you trust me?" He attached his hands to her waist for safekeeping. If he touched any more of her he might not be able to control himself. It had occurred to him more than once that sex with her might ruin him if it didn't work out in the long term.

"I want to," she attested with a nod. "I'm trying."

"I've known you for seventy-two hours and I already care about you. That's never happened to me before. With anyone. Ever. What can I do to make you trust me?"

She ran her fingers through his hair. "You're doing it. Just by being here, by doing this."

"If we keep doing much more of this, I won't be able to stop." He was already as hard as a rock.

He loved the way the corners of her mouth curved slightly before her eyes narrowed and brightened. "Yes, I'm getting that impression."

He planted a quick, solid kiss on her lips. "Do you still want to have dinner? Our reservations aren't until eight. My plan was to have a drink here first. That's why I went to Tahoe City, to pick up the wine. It ended up being more trouble than it was worth."

"Of course I still want to have dinner," she assured him. "We can save the wine for another time." She lifted her chin a notch. "I'm actually kind of glad this happened. I was beginning to think that you were perfect."

"And now?" he humored her.

"Now." She brushed his lips with hers. "I know you are."

CHAPTER SIX

"ALL SET," MIKE ANNOUNCED, returning to her side. "They gave our table away, but another one just opened up."

Delaney shifted her gaze to the crowd of people standing around the entrance to the restaurant. "How'd you manage that?" she asked.

Mike's eyes twinkled impishly. "Got lucky, I guess."

Delaney was sending him an indulgent nod when the hostess appeared. "Right this way, Mr. Savoy." She led them through the dining room and out back, stopping at a table on the edge of the patio not twenty feet from the shore. "Enjoy," she said and retraced her steps.

Delaney shot Mike an astonished look and raised her eyebrows.

"Really lucky." He gestured for her to sit, and much to her delight, pulled the chair on the opposite side of the table around next to hers. "Are you cold?" he asked, draping his arm over the back of her chair. "We can eat inside if you'd rather. It's already cooling down and the sun hasn't even set."

"Oh, no." Sinking into the deep cushion, she watched the edge of the crimson sun cast pastel shadows behind the mountains. The air smelled fresh and sweet, like pine straw and marshmallows braided with bark. "It's beautiful. And the break of the waves is like a symphony."

"You're right, but the scenery is only the half of it." He pressed his lips to hers. "You manage to look more striking every time I see you. Candlelight suits you. "

Delaney could only blush, feeling her stomach jump for the tenth time in an hour.

Just then their waitress arrived. Placing a cocktail napkin in the shape of the lake in front of each of them, she proposed, "Shall we start with some drinks? An appetizer to share?"

Apparently they looked enough like a couple to share an appetizer, Delaney thought, deferring to Mike.

"We'll have a bottle of the Amador County Cabernet and a couple of waters for starters."

"Perrier, sir?"

"Nope. We'll drink from the lake tonight."

The waitress nodded in acknowledgement, then walked away. They turned their attention to the menu and after a few silent beats, Mike commented, "They have a little bit of everything. What looks good?"

"All of it, but I overdid it at the brunch. That was quite a spread."

"As advertised. Brian doesn't do anything halfway. We can order a few small plates, keep it light." He closed his menu as if the matter had been settled and continued, "Did Brian and Lindsay get off on time? He seemed distracted, watching the clock."

"By the skin of their teeth. I think he would have rather bought Lindsay a new wardrobe in Maui than have her pack her suitcase one more time. She wants to look perfect for him every second. I've never seen her so happy."

Mike shook his head in agreement. "Kelsey and I were talking about that earlier."

"It sounds like she and Brian are close even though she lives in San Diego."

"They are. He and his ex-wife have a good relationship as well. None of the drama you hear about sometimes."

"That's wonderful," Delaney said as the waitress served their wine. Then she heard herself say, "I haven't seen my father since I was two years old."

Mike gaped at her over the rim of his wine glass. "Do you even remember him?"

"No." Delaney took a meditative sip of wine. She hadn't talked about this in a long time. "My mother rarely spoke of him. It was just the two of us; we struggled. The scholarship to UC really helped. Mom would have found a way to send me to college, though." Delaney felt a proud smile start in her heart and spread to her mouth. "She wanted me to experience all the things she missed. She was thrilled at the prospect of my having a normal life with Ryan. Unfortunately, that didn't work out."

Mike cleared his throat and shifted a bit in his seat. After a moment, he asked, "Was she a young mother?"

"Yes. My grandparents were very supportive. We lived with them until I was ten. She worked during the day and finished school at night. Once she got on her feet, we moved to the near north side of Chicago so she'd have a shorter commute to work."

"She sounds like a real go-getter."

"She definitely pulled her self up by her bootstraps and got it done. How about you? Did you have a traditional upbringing?"

"You could say that. My parents have been married for fifty years. My mom was typical of her generation; kids, house, car pool. My dad worked the family business until they sold it. Since then, he's played thousands of rounds of golf, attended almost every Giants home game and succeeded in driving my mother nearly insane."

Around a laugh, Delaney asked, "You decided not to go into the family business?"

Mike waved the idea away. "I've been flying since I was sixteen. Earned my engineering degree and logged hours at the same time. I wasn't very social in college. I spent more time in the cockpit than on campus."

"Not me," Delaney told him. "I took it all in. My love affair with California began the moment I stepped off the plane."

"And ended with graduation?"

"Lindsay tried to persuade me to stay out here for graduate school, but four years away from home was long enough. Then I met Ryan and one thing led to another. " Odd that her stomach didn't sink at the mere thought of him anymore.

The food arrived, diverting the conversation. They ate and chatted easily, comparing growing up in the city to suburban San Rafael and being an only child to having four older sisters. Before Delaney knew it, the waitress was offering dessert. They both declined and Mike settled the check.

"How about a walk on the beach?" He suggested as they rose from the table.

"I'd love that," she replied, thrilled that he wasn't in any more of hurry than she was for the evening to end.

Mike took her hand in his and led her out the back exit of the restaurant.

After a few quiet strides, he said, "Want to grab a nightcap or coffee? There's a beach bar with live music up here a bit."

She leaned against his shoulder. "Sure, but I'm happy to just walk on the beach with you. Don't feel like you have to entertain me."

He stopped walking. "That's the thing, I don't. I don't feel obligated or awkward or as if I have to make small talk. It's like I already know everything about you, but I don't. I want to." He curved his hand at the nape of her neck and pinned his lips to hers, setting off fireworks in her stomach. Then he pulled away and went on evenly, "But first I need to know something. I need to know if you're kissing me or a ghost."

◈

No wonder Delaney had been so upset when he was late. Her fiancé wasn't the first man in her life to change his mind and leave her. But that wasn't why Mike felt like someone had tied his stomach into cement knots. She'd said *unfortunately that didn't work out*. Maybe she wasn't over that jerk after all. Maybe she was on the rebound from a two-year losing streak.

Bewilderment replaced the contentment in her eyes and her brow crinkled. Mike gave her a few seconds, and when she came up empty, elaborated, "Earlier you said unfortunately it didn't work out with...Ryan." He bit off the name. "Do you still feel that way? If he walked back into your life right now, would you take him back?" He felt as if he couldn't take another breath until she answered.

Awareness rippled across her face and her lips formed silent syllables. She placed an unsteady hand on his face. "No, of course not. I wouldn't be here with you, like this, if I would. There was a time when I would have taken him back. But not anymore. Not even before he got married last year. That's when I realized it wasn't marriage he was running from, it was me." She dropped her hand to her side and turned toward the water. "And that was even more humbling than being left at the altar."

Mike wanted to kill this guy. If she were his he would love her, cherish her, never let her go. He hugged her from behind. "He's the one who should be humbled. I'm sorry if I upset you. I had to make sure I wasn't the rebound guy. You know, the one you test the waters with after almost drowning."

Delaney rested her head in the crook of his shoulder. "No, you're the one who made me want to go back in the water again. And I'm already drowning." She gulped. "In you."

Relief washing over him, Mike spun her around. "Laney, I'm drowning too. We can save each other." He placed the palms of his hands on her face and kissed her long and hard, as if to seal the deal. Her eyes were shinning like diamonds in the darkness. But it was her hair, like that of a chestnut mare, that he loved the most. He wanted to run his fingers through it over and over while thoroughly exploring her mouth with his. From there he would lick his way down to the firm, round breasts that had crushed against him last night. And were peeking out of her shirt right now, tempting him. "I want to spend the night with you. I want to wake up with you tomorrow." And the next day, he surprised himself by thinking.

She grabbed his wrists. "I want that too. But—"

"But tonight won't be that night," he interrupted her. "Because the first time I make love to you has to be right for both of us. When your eyes are full of anticipation and abandon, not apprehension and uncertainty." He rested his forehead against hers and let out a mollifying breath. "So let me know. I'm ready whenever you are."

⁕

Delaney had seen eyes full of lust before. But never like this. The ones frantically searching hers held a need bordering on desperation. A need willing to be checked until she was ready. Mike assumed they would make love; it was simply a matter of time.

"Let's go this way." He slipped his hand back into hers and started walking. "My grandparents had a house around here. I wonder if I can find it in the dark."

She could only gawk at him as the coarse sand invaded her flip flops. No pressure, no guilt, no abrupt end to the evening?

"It was close to Kings Beach," Mike was saying. "In a wooded area, but still lakefront." He took in the lake as if conjuring up the memory. "I remember counting the steps down to the dock and my sisters burying me in the sand."

Delaney relaxed a little. "Sounds like you had a wonderful, normal childhood."

He shrugged, then answered offhandedly. "Whatever normal is."

"More normal than a girl who never knew her father."

After a thoughtful pause Mike asked, "Do you ever wonder about him?"

"I used to. If he was still alive, what he looked like, what he did for a living. Mom spoon-fed me bits and pieces of information. To satisfy my curiosity, I guess."

"Or to protect you."

"Maybe. He'd been in trouble with the law at one point. I remember a detective coming to the house. We had no information to offer; it had been a decade since we'd heard from him. For all I know, he's spent his life in prison." She looked over at Mike in wonder. "I don't think I've ever told anyone that before."

He gave her hand a supportive squeeze, encouraging her to go on.

"When I got older, I realized I was born and raised in love, but not conceived in it. Mom didn't want me to make the same mistake she did." She managed a regretful smile. "Instead I made a different one."

Mike stopped walking and pulled her to him. "You didn't make the mistake. He did. And I plan to make the most of it, if you'll let me."

She could do nothing but nod, in complete awe of him. There was something different about the way he held her, kissed her. Beyond her heart soaring in her chest and stomach tugging. There was a familiarity, a sense of belonging. Like finally settling down after years of moving. Or finding the right job after bouncing around from one to another. Or meeting the right man. A man who lived two thousand miles away. Who came from a solid, presumably upstanding family. What would they think of a girl raised by a single mother who went to college on a wing and a prayer? Chances are things wouldn't get that far anyway. No matter how sincere Mike was, why would he commit to a long-distance relationship with a woman he'd known for only a few days? He probably had women falling at his feet, who would jump into bed with him without a second thought. Yet, he was here with her, willing to let her take the reins, set the pace.

They walked hand in hand in companionable silence for a while, past the estates that lined the increasingly rocky shore, the docks the held their boats and jet skis. The second or third homes of the ultra-wealthy investment bankers, tech giants, celebrities from San Francisco, L.A. and beyond. Here and there were some high-end condo and townhouse rentals, hotels, restaurants. The night was quiet but for the boats rocking on the waves and the occasional call of a bird signing off for the day. Stars peppered the crushed velvet-like sky, illuminating the Sierras just enough to cast shadows on the sleeping basin.

"I think this is it," Mike said, stopping in front of a huge chalet-style house, with wraparound decks on all three levels and a dock large enough to accommodate both boats tied to it. Amber lights burned from behind unobstructed ceiling-to-floor windows and landscape lighting illuminated the generous yard and garden walkways.

Delaney was blown away. "This was your grandparents' house?"

Mike considered a moment. "I'm pretty sure. But the steps used to be wood not stone." He assessed the property discerningly. "I'd like to come back during the day, from the water, to get a better look. I heard it was up for sale. There's no signage so it's likely a pocket listing." Then he turned to her, asking "What are you doing tomorrow?"

Delaney returned his boyish grin. "I think I'm going swimming."

CHAPTER SEVEN

MIKE COULDN'T READ THE clock on the dresser, but since the sun was protruding through the heavily lined curtains of his room, he guessed it was at least eight o'clock. Or maybe a little later, he decided, as the squeaky wheels of a cleaning cart gave way to a door slamming and then a diminishing conversation.

If only Jessica had been so easily dismissed.

He hadn't taken note of the number before answering, hoping it was Delaney calling to say she wanted him to come back. He'd very reluctantly left her at Lindsay's front door after some hot and heavy kisses good night. He didn't want to rush her, but he couldn't take much more of this back and forth. They'd made a date for today, starting with breakfast and then a day on the lake. But secretly he'd hoped she'd find herself suffering as much as he was and call him. He'd extended his reservation through Tuesday morning and even played a couple hands of blackjack before going upstairs, betting more on her libido than the dealer having a bad night.

He'd lost both wagers.

Instead it was Jessica. Drunk, horny and wanting to know when he'd be in town again. She hadn't seen him, or anyone else from the sound of it, in months. Since she probably wouldn't remember anyway, Mike informed her that he was on the Dallas rotation for the next two weeks. No plans to be in Chicago—at least not yet. It wasn't until the third call that he firmly reminded her that they were no longer seeing each other. He'd also managed to dodge her inquiry as to his availability. It would be his luck that even in a city the size of Chicago, Delaney and Jessica would have a mutual friend or other connection. Most likely though, a zip code was all they shared. They were polar opposites.

Jessica was bleach blonde, unabashedly lascivious and recently divorced when they met. She had no interest in a relationship, so their living two time zones apart presented no problem. They had a mutually beneficial thing going until she started comparing him unfavorably to her ex-husband. Mike wasn't sure if she was trying to make him jealous or contemplating reconciliation. Either way, he wanted no part of it. They went their separate ways and he hadn't heard from her since.

Until last night.

Powering on his phone, he discovered that she'd called seven times in total. He deleted the messages without listening to them. He needed to shower and pick up breakfast. He promised Delaney he'd call if he was running late, which he was since it was close to nine o'clock.

"Good morning." Her voice was low, alluring, sexy. It was the first time they'd spoken on the phone.

"Good morning. Did I wake you?"

"No. I've been up, working."

"Working? I thought you were taking a few days off."

"Technically. But I've got a big presentation on Thursday."

Mike ignored the beep of an incoming call. "Are you still up for the beach? Maybe a boat or jet ski ride?" He wondered if she heard the hopefulness in his voice.

"Sure. Are you?" Her tone mirrored his now.

He felt a grin narrow his eyes. "Of course. But I just woke up. I won't be there for about an hour. I'll grab coffee and something to eat on the way. Any requests?"

"Whatever you're having will be fine."

All he wanted was her. "I'll hold you to that. See you in a bit."

There was dead air for a few seconds. Then she said, "Mike?"

"Yeah?"

"Thanks for calling."

Baby steps were better than standing still, Mike inwardly reasoned. Somehow he would make her trust him. "I can't wait to see you, Laney."

There was another pause. Then in a voice laced with struggle, she said, "I can't wait to see you, either. Hurry."

❧

Delaney was still smiling what her mother would call a stupid smile when the phone rang again a few minutes later.

"She lives!"

"Very funny."

"Having an empty inbox this morning was one thing, but to not hear from you by noon?"

Avery McGovern's voice was overly dramatic. "I was afraid you fell in the lake. It's one of the deeper ones in the country if I remember my middle school geography correctly."

"Your memory serves you well," Delaney told her assistant through a chuckle. "It's the second deepest, inched out by Crater Lake in Oregon."

After a few silent beats, Avery put in, "Wow."

Delaney unwound her hair from the Velcro roller. She felt like she was in high school again, getting all dolled up to go to the beach. "Wow, what?"

"I can't remember the last time I heard you laugh like that."

And Avery would know. The women had met almost a decade ago as interns at Hudson and Grace. But unlike Delaney, Avery had no desire to move up the corporate ladder. She was buying her time until a baby came along and she left the working world behind.

"How was the wedding?" Avery was asking. "Lindsay?"

"Perfect and more perfect. I hope you enjoyed your reprieve. I'm doing e-mails right now. Then I'll get cranking on fine-tuning my presentation."

"You'll nail it. You always do." Her voice trailed off as if addressing a matter at hand, then piped up again. "You haven't missed a thing around here. Summer finally arrived. Do you need anything checked at your apartment? I can catch the train from there just as easily."

"No. But eventually I'll need help crunching numbers. I'll call you."

"Okay." She hesitated, then said, "Laney?"

"Yeah?"

"Whatever you're doing out there, keep doing it. You sound like the Delaney I used to know. The one who had a glass of wine at lunch and secretly slipped off her heels under the table at meetings. The one whose laugh was contagious and whose smile lit up the room. That's the Delaney I've missed. That's the Delaney who'll be a great vice-president. Not the gaunt one with bags under her eyes who insists she's fine but is really just going through the motions. Or the workaholic who refuses to delegate because she somehow has to fill every waking moment of her life so she doesn't have to live it."

Delaney sat in stunned silence, staring at her reflection in the full-length mirror. Avery was absolutely right. She hadn't been herself in so long that she'd forgotten who she was. She'd been hiding from herself, from her life. And now she'd found herself again in the last place she could have expected. On a trip she'd almost talked herself out of taking. At a wedding she could have justified missing. In a man she hadn't known a week ago.

"Are you there?" Avery's voice faltered a bit. "I mean that in a good way. I've been worried about you. We all have."

"I know," Delaney told her from the heart. "Thanks for that. And for calling to check on me."

"Sure. I'll talk to you tomorrow."

"Avery?" Delaney caught her just in time.

"Yeah?"

"I've missed her too."

"Well, then, welcome back. It's been way too long."

The women disconnected and wrapping her bikini-clad body in a blanket, Delaney walked outside. The upstairs deck allowed her a panoramic view of the lake and the Sierras in the distance. The water was a sheet of cobalt glass, and the beach was empty but for the gaggle of geese making their morning trek across the freshly raked sand. She inhaled the brisk morning air and felt the corners of her mouth curve upward. Mike was on his way, despite her sending him away last night with only kisses at the door. Truth was that if he'd pushed her, she might have invited him in. Instead, she'd fallen asleep pretending she was wrapped in his arms, with the scent of him in her hair and the taste of him on her lips.

She walked back inside and traded the blanket for shorts and a sweatshirt. Returning to the mirror, she applied mascara to the eyes her father had apparently given her. Did he ever wonder about her? Who she'd become? Where life had taken her? Obviously not. Thanks to the internet, all that information was at his fingertips. And at hers. Straightening the bed, Delaney took in the room. Lindsay had spared no expense in remodeling, even in the guest bedroom. The linens were as thick and plush as the finest hotel. Like the Fairmont, where she had yet to cancel her reservation.

Her gaze shifted to the laptop on the bed. She could take care of that right now, with a quick call or click. After all, spending a few carefree days together in Tahoe was one thing. Dropping herself smack dab in the middle of Mike's life via Brian's apartment was another. She was still debating that dilemma when a firm knock sounded below. Cautious optimism and girlish enthusiasm wrangling in her stomach, Delaney hurried downstairs. She smoothed her hair and took a deep breath, then opened the door.

Mike was standing there with a brown paper bag in one hand and a cup carrier in the other. A broad grin stretched across his face. "Hi."

Knees turning into rubber, Delaney returned the smile. "Hi. Here, let me take something."

"I've got it," he assured her. The earthy smell of coffee mingled with the spicy leather scent of his cologne. Closing the door, she followed him into the kitchen.

"I wasn't sure if you drank regular or decaf, so I got both." He presented her with two paper cups.

"Regular."

He gave her the cup in his right hand, then delved into the bag, coming out with two bundles. "The last two cinnamon swirl coffee cakes. And the woman behind me was none too happy about it." He flashed a devilish smile. "She was still complaining when I left."

"Umm. My favorite," she delighted, beginning to unwrap the wax paper.

"First things first." Mike quieted her hands and pulled her to him. "I missed you."

As if instinctual, her arms girdled his neck as she fell into the kiss. And the next. Those fireworks were erupting in the pit of her stomach again, shooting arrows of want through her. That happened every time he touched her, she realized as excitement laced with apprehension spiraled through the want. She broke away, wondering if the heat sweeping through her had taken hold in her cheeks. "I guess so. That was quite a hello."

"Not really, considering I've been thinking about you since the second I woke up."

She searched his eyes, so sure and true, and confessed, "I've been thinking about you too."

He nuzzled her neck. "I wanted you there with me." She tilted her head back as his tongue made tiny circles down her throat. His hands left her waist and ventured under the sweatshirt, tentatively at first. Then, sensing no resistance, he cupped her breasts and began caressing her nipples through the bikini top. "I wanted my hands on you."

"I love your hands on me," she muttered. "That's what I was thinking about when I woke up. All the places they've been."

She heard his sharp intake of breath before he righted his head and scooped her up, setting her down on the countertop. Leveling their eyes, he flattened his palms on the granite. "Where else can I put my hands? There are so many places I want them to be. But once I let them go, I might not be able to stop myself from taking you. I care about you too much to do that. Unless you're ready to be with me."

The lust, the raw want, was back in his eyes again, but it was peppered with something more profound. Delaney drew a recuperative breath. "I want that too. I don't want to lose you. But I can't survive something like that again."

He pushed himself off the kitchen island and started to pace. "Is that what you think? That I'm going to make love to you and then just take off? Or that if you don't sleep with me soon, you'll never see me again?" He looked at her through eyes full of disappointment. "Is that who you think I am?"

She watched him blaze a trail across the wood floor. "No, of course not. I—"

"If that were all that mattered, I wouldn't be here today," he cut her off. "If that were all that mattered, I wouldn't care if you were on the rebound." His phone started ringing in his pocket, only adding to his frustration. "If that were all that mattered," he drew it out and nodded as if to confirm a suspicion, "I would answer this. It's about the tenth time she's called in as many hours."

Delaney felt her stomach take a nosedive, somehow suctioning all the air from her lungs. The waves of desire were replaced by curls of nausea. Hopping down, she crossed her arms over her chest to brace herself against the impending pain. "She?"

His eyes fired with regret, not the guilt Delaney expected. Mike threw the phone down on the counter and rubbed the back of his neck. "I shouldn't have said that. One has nothing to do with the other." Returning to her, he gripped her forearms. "See what I mean? I can barely think straight, let alone put a sentence together anymore. That's how much you get to me. How much you're come to mean to me in only a few days. No one has ever mattered to me like this before."

Not giving the admission its proper due, Delaney stiffened, asking, "Who is she, Mike?" Whoever she was, he had slept or was sleeping with her. Recently enough for her to call repeatedly, knowing he would eventually answer. And come back for more.

Taking two steps backward, he started with a sigh. "Jessica and I had a relationship for about a year. I haven't seen or spoken to her in months." He stalled, then begrudged, "Until last night."

The wretchedness in Delaney's stomach snaked through her body and settled in her chest. She could feel all the life draining out of her, leaving only a boneless puddle of dread. "Last night?" While she was laying in bed, wishing Mike was holding her, was he thinking about someone else? Someone who unlike her, had no qualms about casual, meaningless sex.

Mike resumed pacing. "When my phone rang, I didn't even look at the caller ID, assuming it was you."

"Me?"

"I was hoping you'd reconsidered, wanted me to come back. But it was Jessica. She was drunk and amorous and wanting to know when I was coming back into town."

"Back to San Francisco?"

"Chicago, of all places," he explained with a low grunt. "Her brother and I have been on parallel rotations for years. She and I…connected at a Christmas party a couple of years ago. That led to a few layover meet-ups, an occasional long weekend." He paused, then finished with care, "No commitment."

"So it was just sex?"

His nod was tight-lipped and subtle. "Shallow as it sounds. She never visited me in San Francisco. We saw each other in Chicago or Dallas. Her schedule was almost as hectic as mine."

Delaney tried to act unimpressed. "So what happened?"

Mike shrugged his shoulders. "It got too complicated." Returning to her, he tipped her chin and found her eyes. "Laney, she has nothing to do with us. Even if I hadn't met you, I wouldn't see her again."

A little steadier now, Delaney suggested, "Shouldn't you tell her that? So she'll stop calling you?" And because it would make her feel better, selfish as that was.

"I tried! Three times! Realizing it was futile and you were in for the night, I turned off my phone and went to sleep. She left four messages in the interim."

"But today she is sober. You could reason with her." Explain that you met someone, Delaney silently added.

"That's easier said than done," Mike said with a defeated shake of the head. "Besides, I don't want to waste this beautiful day dealing with Jessica. I want to spend it with you. Okay?"

"Okay," Delaney agreed half-heartedly.

Mike cocked his head to the side for a moment, as if weighing the pros and cons of his decision. Then he reached around her, grabbed his phone, and contended, "That doesn't sound like okay." His tone was serious, but ribbons of satisfaction had crept into his eyes, like her discontentedness pleased him. "So we'll make a call." He tapped the screen, then held the phone between their heads.

Delaney was appalled. "Mike, no!" The last thing she wanted to do was to talk to this woman.

He held his hand up in the air as the phone rang steadily.

A low, husky voice answered on the third ring. "Hi there, Cowboy. Where have you been? I've been trying to reach you."

Shooting Delaney a wry look, Mike said assuredly, "I can see that. Don't you remember our little talk last night? Or had you killed too many brain cells by then?"

"I remember some of it. Especially the part about meeting up in Dallas next week. I've missed you, Mike. Don't you miss me?"

He cast his eyes to the sky and put a troubled hand on his forehead. "Jess, we agreed our relationship had run its course. It's time you found someone else to have fun with."

"I've tried," Jessica admitted with a long sigh. "But none of them are as good in bed as you are." She paused, then added roguishly, "You are no doubt in the same boat. Or so I'm told."

Having heard enough, Delaney started to walk away.

Mike grabbed her arm, pulling her back. "Keep looking." He stroked her cheek with the back of his hand. "I've met someone."

Delaney's breath caught in her throat and she managed a small smile.

"That's not what you said last night," Jessica purred. "Not that I mind either way."

"I mind." Mike told her, his voice a little harder now. "And we both know I didn't invite you to meet me in Dallas. 'A' for effort, though. It's over. Are we clear?"

"I suppose," Jessica answered effortlessly. "But keep my number handy. I plan to do the same with yours."

"Suit yourself. Goodbye, Jess."

Delaney looked on as Mike deleted the number from his contacts and call history. He turned off his phone and slid it into his pocket. "Satisfied? You don't have to sleep with me to keep me around. If that were all I wanted, she would be my first call."

"Obviously," Delaney returned, sniffing the air.

"Laney, look at me." He brought her face back to his. "The next time I make love will be the first time I make love with you. It will be the first of many times. A time when I can hold you for the rest of the night. And wake up and make love to you again. A time when you want me just as much as I want you, not because you're afraid of losing me." He brushed his lips against hers and joined their foreheads. "Until then, I'll have to wait."

CHAPTER EIGHT

THE HOTEL HAD PLENTY of jet skis to rent, but Delaney didn't want her own. That was a problem, Mike discovered as the cool spray showered their legs. Because as much as he loved having hers pressed against his, he couldn't shake the thought of them parted beneath him.

A ski boat came into view, ending Mike's reverie. Cutting left, he sped up and steered them deeper into the blue haze, feeling her grip around his middle tighten. They headed east, hugging the rocky shore lined with mansions built of glass and framed in wood, until they came upon a cove where a cluster of boats were anchored. Mindful of the giant boulders skimming the surface, Mike killed the engine. "Do you want to dock here? I could tie up to one of those lines," he suggested over his shoulder, pointing accordingly. "We can swim around here or go in to the shore."

"Sure." Delaney peered over the side, astonishing, "The fusion of blues here is breathtaking. Almost preternatural."

"And on a day like today, with wall-to-wall sunshine, it's limpid to seventy feet," Mike informed her, removing the key and jumping in. If nothing else, the sixty-eight degree water would cool him off. On the outside anyway. He retrieved the rope from the rear compartment, then swam to a boat anchored nearby.

"Need a tow?" the tanned, heavyset skipper called from the bow.

"Just a spot to tie up for a bit."

The other man waved an agreeable hand in the air. "Go ahead. We'll be here all afternoon."

"Thanks." Mike made a few quick knots. When he returned, Delaney was already in the water.

"Do I really have to wear this thing?" she attempted pleadingly. "I can swim."

"There's a difference between swimming and being thrown off a jet ski into the middle of a lake with which you're not familiar."

"Then it's all settled," she decided, unzipping the life jacket. "I'm already in the lake, so this stays here." She hung the vest on the handles. "Where to?"

Mike had to admire her tenacity in spite of himself. "Let's swim to shore. Sand Harbor has the best sand in the basin. Something about the prevailing winds."

They swam a few strokes side by side. When Delaney could touch, Mike took her hand and they began trudging through the pebble-lined lakebed in their water shoes. "This is where I used to swim when I was a kid. There were years when we stayed up here all summer and my dad would come up on the weekends."

"You must miss it."

"I do. That's why I've been thinking about buying a place. Even before I got wind of my grandparents' house being available. I was supposed to be doing that today; looking at real estate." He shot her a clever look. "But I got a better offer."

"Me too. I should be working." She hesitated, then went on, "So, are you really looking at something as large as that?"

She was so cute, he thought, and too polite to inquire as to his ability to afford such a property, especially as a second home. She didn't know what she didn't know. "I'm open to it. I'm also considering a condo or townhouse. As an investment and a weekend getaway." With you, he almost said.

She nodded in acknowledgement and he wondered if she had had the same thought. After a few silent steps, Mike gestured to the bowl-shaped outdoor theater nestled between the shore and tree line. "There are plays and concerts here all summer. If we had another night here, that would be fun." He gave up trying to keep his hands to himself and pulled her close. "I wish we had another night. Here or anywhere else."

"Me, too."

They stood there for a long moment, with the shallow water lapping at their ankles. Finally Mike swallowed hard and said, "What's your schedule next week? I'm only a few blocks from the Fairmont."

"I'm not staying at the Fairmont next week," she stated with a ragged breath. Her voice was small, like it had been when they were discussing Jessica.

"You're not?"

She shook her head from side to side.

Mike felt his stomach drop. "Are you going home early?"

"No." She raised her hand to stroke his hair. "Not until Sunday."

Mike relaxed a little. "As much as I'd love for you to stay with me, I'm afraid that's a bit premature. Where are you staying?"

"Lindsay offered me the apartment," she informed him. "She thinks I'll be more comfortable there. And then someone will be there at least part of the —"

Before she could finish, Mike picked her up and spun her around. "Laney, that's great!"

"It is?"

"Of course!" He set her back down, thrilled at the prospect of her being right next door. "Why wouldn't it be?"

"I don't want you to feel obligated to see me. It's pretty hard to avoid your next door neighbor."

"The last thing I want to do is avoid you." He ran his hands up and down her arms. "I want you more than ever. How can I make you believe that?"

"I want to. I'm starting to," she told him with borrowed conviction.

It couldn't be soon enough for Mike. Because despite the dip in the lake, the fire inside him was raging again. And he was exhausted from fighting it alone. "Good. Because I don't just want to make love with you, Laney. I'm in love with you."

❧

Colton did a three-sixty, then looked over his right shoulder again for good measure. This part of the river valley was still untouched by man, probably protected within an inch of its life by the tree huggers. California had served him well that way, he laughed to himself. But that was the only way, he reflected remorsefully, trying to catch his breath. He banged an aggravated fist against his chest. Damn heartburn. Gets worse every time.

He pulled the shovel off his back and began to dig. He'd buried it here among the pines and brush for safekeeping. And now after a dozen years, two buses and an afternoon of walking in the blazing sun, he wanted it for a completely different reason. He'd barely been getting by when he took that job. Figured Sansome wouldn't miss a few hundred large here and there. Soon enough he would find out if he had. And he had to be ready.

CHAPTER NINE

SITTING AT THE TOLL booth on the Golden Gate Bridge the next night, Delaney let out a wistful sigh. No matter how many times she'd seen the pastel sky fade away and the twinkling lights of San Francisco illuminate the night, she was awed. Almost as awed as she was when Mike professed to being in love with her. No, she corrected herself, she'd been floored. Because it's ridiculous to be in love with someone you hardly know, isn't it?

It was a question that had occupied her ruminating mind all night. After a fitful attempt at sleep, she'd finally risen before daybreak with the intention of working. Yet even the most important presentation of her career couldn't compete with Mike's proclamation. It filled her with an joy so indescribable, she felt like she was walking on air. But that does not a VP of Marketing make.

Their day on the water had ended with take-out and wine on Lindsay's lower deck. They'd never made it back to the California side of the lake to get a better look at Mike's grandparents' old house. Instead, they'd spent much of the afternoon sunning on the rocks at Sand Harbor and swimming among the other boaters and jet skiers. Delaney was amazed at how crowded it was for a Monday. Mike laughed that off, saying that most people at the lake in the summertime were on "Tahoe Time."

He'd left first thing this morning, leaving her the day to work. He'd texted her goodbye, likely assuming she was still sleeping, around seven. When she replied, he immediately called her, wishing her a productive day and safe drive to San Francisco. He would figure something out for them for dinner. He really was in love with her. She could hear it in his voice.

Using the Lombard exit, she debated taking Broadway and dealing with heavy traffic or Washington where parked cars often packed the narrow street. She went with the former and promptly got stuck behind a delivery truck. Swearing under her breath, she was lifting her eyes to the rearview mirror when her phone rang.

"Where are you?" Mike wanted to know.

"On Broadway and Polk behind a truck." She looked out the window. "And next to a bus. I thought the air out here was supposed to be cleaner than Chicago. I'm surrounded by pollution."

"We don't have cleaner air, just laws to make us think we do," he explained dryly. "If you can get to Hyde, take it south to Washington. Jackson is one way going west there. Come back north on Leavenworth. I'll meet you."

Faint cheering in the background subsided, like he had turned off a game on TV.

"You don't have to do that, Mike. I can find my way."

"I know I don't have to. I want to. Twenty-two hours is long enough. I'll see you a few minutes," he said, then disconnected.

Delaney lost her breath. Mike had counted the hours since he'd seen her. She made her way to Hyde and within ten minutes he was in sight, wearing jeans and a San Francisco Giants sweatshirt. She pulled into the parking garage, stopping at his silent direction and rolled down the window.

"Hi," he greeted, leaning down and pressing his lips to hers. "Pull in behind me." He pointed to a stall over to the left. "I moved my car all the way up since I won't need it for a few days."

He owns two spots, Delaney marveled, complying. She no sooner had the car in park than he was at her side again. He helped her out and folded her into his arms. "I thought you'd never get here."

His embrace was as welcoming as a warm bed on a frigid night. "I was working." Or trying to, she inwardly added. "I didn't expect you to be waiting."

He leaned back just enough to make eye contact. "Well, I was."

Her heart skipped a beat. "I'm sorry. I'm not used to having someone waiting for me."

"Get used to it," he said, bringing his lips to hers.

His mouth was cool and minty, but his tongue were searing hot. He maneuvered her against the side of the car, still knocking as hard as the engine Mike had sent revving inside her. His weight was on her for the first time, she realized. And she liked it.

Releasing her with a reluctant breath, he grabbed her bag from the backseat saying, "I hope you're hungry. I ordered Chinese." He wrapped his arm around her waist and led her through the parking garage to the elevator. "It should be here anytime."

She was suddenly disturbingly hungry. But not for Chinese. "Great," she responded, drawing a calming breath.

They rode in companionable silence to the eighth floor. Mike stopped at the second door on the right and began punching numbers into a keypad. "While you get settled, I'll grab the food and meet you at my place," he said, nodding toward the door they'd just passed.

The locks clicked and Mike held the door open, gesturing for her to enter. The apartment was done in black and tans, with unadorned windows making up most of the walls. "Kelsey's room is over here," he informed her, walking through the stainless steel kitchen and down a shadowed hallway. "The lights out there are on timers, but not in here," he called from somewhere in the back as a beam of light appeared. "I'll put your bag on the bed." Still talking, he reappeared. "I'm going down to wait for the delivery guy. If you beat me over there, my code is my parents' anniversary, five-three-six-eight."

She wondered if the flash of admiration at the sweet sentiment was noticeable on her face. "Okay. Thanks."

After he left, Delaney walked over to the window and contemplated the bustling street below. Where Mike had been waiting for her. Something he'd told her to get used to. She could certainly get used to having his arms around her. But would they catch her if she let herself fall? Delaney could count her stable of lovers on one hand. All of whom she'd known for longer than a week. None of whom's slightest touch launched rockets in her stomach. Or whose fleeting kisses made her wick with moisture below. But with whom, she allowed for the first time, she'd fallen helplessly in love. Pushing back the fear, she let out a deep breath and willed herself the courage to find out.

CHAPTER TEN

THE WORDS HAD CROSSED his lips without warning, and Delaney hadn't returned them. But she was here, he reminded himself, unloading the take-out boxes on the kitchen counter. She could have stayed in Tahoe until tomorrow, or kept her reservation at the Fairmont. But she'd chosen to work from here instead. Progress.

He'd been in love before, of course. But never like this. First he'd attributed it to her unassuming beauty and innate affability. Then the thrill of the chase; she wasn't one to jump into bed with anyone, like Jessica and some of the women he knew of late. But it was more than that. There was something about the way she looked at him, the way he stirred inside when he held her. She was like a tune he couldn't shake. Not that he wanted to.

She was still tentative about him though and he couldn't blame her. It enraged Mike to think of her on her wedding day, no doubt looking positively gorgeous, waiting for the cowardly ass to show. The dread she must have felt when she realized he wasn't coming. He slammed the cabinet door, rattling the dishes along with his disposition. And when a knock sounded on the door a few minutes later, he was still in that frame of mind.

Until he saw her.

"Hi," she said around a smile, handing him the bottle of wine in her hand.

"Hi." Carnal thoughts replaced the indignation as he ushered her in. "I was just doling everything out."

She looked around appraisingly for a few seconds, then said, "Mike, this is incredible.

Especially by San Francisco standards."

"Thanks," he replied, leading her into the kitchen. "I wanted a panorama of the city and of the bay. So I bought two apartments, one corner and one interior. The renovation was a nightmare, took forever and went way over budget. But even a native San Franciscan like me can't dispute the view."

"It's absolutely stunning."

"It certainly is." He brought her to him. "You look even more beautiful than you did in Tahoe. I didn't think that was possible."

"I've never felt more beautiful than I do when you hold me." She let out a decisive breath. "I fell asleep last night in a sweatshirt, imagining your arms wrapped around me."

Mike couldn't help but laugh. "If you were in my arms in bed last night, you wouldn't have been wearing a sweatshirt." He wondered if she had any idea how much she got to him. He brushed her lips with his. "I really missed you."

Putting her arms around his neck, she returned a deeper kiss. "I missed you, too."

Her mouth was like a conduit, sending a static charge from her body to his. Starting at his lips, it manifested itself into a tense wire and crackled through him like lightning, settling in his cock. He didn't just want her, he ached for her. Being in her proximity was an unnerving dichotomy of gratification and torture. It was becoming increasingly difficult to keep himself in check and not give into the animalistic-like yearning that threatened his sense of decency.

Knowing he couldn't bury himself in her, he buried his face in her hair and managed to choke out, "We should probably eat. The food is getting cold."

"Yeah, we should," she said breathlessly.

"Laney..."

"Mike. Come back to me."

He obliged, meeting her doe-like eyes. The conflicted passion he'd seen in them before was gone, replaced by something more solicitous. She leaned up and kissed him, taking his whole mouth this time. He felt the moan in her throat as her lips parted and their tongues found one another. Her fingers raked through his hair while their mouths gave and took, bit and pulled. With heaving breaths, Mike tore away and made a path with his tongue from her earlobe down her neck and into the valley between her breasts. She tasted bittersweet, like spring flowers mixed with the alcohol in her perfume. She held his head in the palms of her hands as his tongue explored her cleavage and his thumbs caressed her nipples through the thin cotton of her blouse. They hardened in his wake and he felt her body go limp. She leaned against the kitchen island for ballast as her head tipped back in rapture.

His hands left her breasts and rounded to the nape of her neck. He had to see what was under that halter. He wanted her breasts in his hands, her nipples in his mouth, her naked chest pressing against his. Finding the knot, he made quick work of the tie. The strings tumbled down, stopping just below her shoulders. To his delight, he saw no evidence of a bra. Her checks were flushed, her hair was falling in sexy, disheveled waves around her face, her skin damp. Her eyes were hanging onto to his as if by a thread. And glistening with tears.

What the hell was wrong with him?

He jerked back a few steps and bent over, resting his hands on his thighs just above his knees. "Laney, I'm sorry," he panted. "I overstepped my bounds."

"I'm not." She was panting too. She swallowed hard as if steeling herself, then said, "I've been thinking about what you said. About falling in love with someone in a few days."

Hope spooled with the want in his gut. "You have?"

She nodded. "Yeah. I don't think you can."

Mike's stomach fell to his feet, somehow preventing his heart from beating.

A sheepish smile was creeping across her mouth as she came to him. "I know you can.

Because I've fallen madly in love with you, Mike. And I'm sorry I was too much of a coward to tell you that before."

Relief washed over him and he felt his heart resume its normal rhythm. "Laney—"

"Can we try it again?" she interrupted him. "Especially the part about wanting to make love to me. If you still want me, that is."

He lifted a grateful hand to her cheek. "Laney, I don't just want to make love to you. I'm in with love you. You're all I want."

Her eyes filled with shimmer and her breath caught. "Prove it."

"Gladly." He pressed his mouth to hers, then picked her up and carried her into the bedroom. He laid her down on the bed and ranged himself beside her. He skimmed her bare chest with his fingertips, debating where to begin. Her eyes were soft and shiny, but still held a ribbon of reservation. "It it doesn't have to be tonight," he reassured her. "I'll wait as long as it takes."

"I want it to be tonight. It's just that I'm a little out of practice. I don't want to disappoint you."

"How could I be disappointed? The woman I'm in love with wants me. I wanted her from the moment I saw her. And every moment since."

Her gaze was dreamy now. "Then make love to me, Mike," she implored, slipping her hands under his shirt and running her hands up his chest.

"I thought you'd never ask." He quieted her hands with his. "But I want to see all of you first." He slid the halter over her head, jettisoning it to the floor and discovering that his suspicions about the bra had been correct. "You made it easy for me, huh?"

She laughed a little. "Built-in bra. Serendipitous, I guess."

"My lucky day." He touched her mouth gently with his, then kissed his way down to the delicate skin between her breasts. "You're even more beautiful than I imagined." He suckled one breast, then the other as she arched beneath him. "I can't wait to make love to you."

"You don't have to." She reached for him.

He had to somehow pace himself. He pushed her hand away. "Not yet. Once you touch me, I won't be able to control myself."

She looked him dead in the eye. "I don't want you to control yourself."

He didn't want to scare her by saying that actually she did. "Not this time. Not our first time." His hands left her breasts and slid downward. Her skin was soft and smooth and tingled with anticipation like a rose after a sun shower. He found the waistband of her jeans and she wiggled out of them, meeting the same fate as her top. The black lace triangle at the crux between her legs made his cock surge with want. He circled her belly button with his tongue, then licked her pelvis from hipbone to hipbone. She purred his name as he made his way back to her mouth.

Their eyes exchanged a silent message and this time when her hand found his zipper Mike didn't stop her. He wondered if she knew how torturously slow her hands were moving. Kicking off his jeans, he whipped the sweatshirt over his head and returned to her. He laid his body on hers, their legs entangled, the black lace all that separated them. He brushed the errant strands of hair away from her face, telling her, "This time is going to be fast; I've thought of little else for the last five days. More like having sex than making love. But the next time and every time after that will be making love."

She looked into his eyes, and surely saw the other side of his heart, the bottom of his soul. "Not for me. Every time I'm with you will be making love. Sex is what it was before you."

Mike was speechless, in complete and total awe of her. He wanted to tell her he'd never felt this way before, that he wanted to be her last lover and she his. But he didn't want to scare her, rush her. Her hands found his and she guided them to the thin strings at her hips. Together they pushed the lace down and off. The tip of his erection was nudging at her clean-shaven triangle and she parted her legs in welcome. Mike dipped a finger inside her and found her wetness so erotic that he had to take a moment to collect himself. His fingers began to explore her inside and out; first one, then two. Her body seemed to come alive in his hands. She grew wetter with each thrust, digging her nails into his back as she squirmed beneath him, groaning in pleasure. And it was that sexy, guttural sound that sent Mike over the edge of want to need. It was time to fall. Together.

He entered her with a moan of satisfaction that blended seamlessly with her low cries of passion as she tightened around him. Mike tried to resist the urge to thrust too hard, but his thirst for her was insatiable and the animal in him took over. Rocking above her, he drove himself deeper and deeper into her soaking center. She raised her hips to meet his and he felt her orgasm build, release, begin to build again. And when she gazed up at him, her eyes full of love and abandon, Mike could hold out no more. Heart flying out of his chest, he exploded into her, making love for the first time.

❧

"Am I crushing you?" Mike raised up on his elbows

"Hmm?" Delaney had never experienced such an intense orgasm before. Her body was still vibrating. "Oh, no. I love having your weight on me."

Mike gave her a suspicious look. "You sure? Because you seem a little shell-shocked. Did I hurt you?"

Her throat tightened. He was so sweet, so earnest. And so worried he'd hurt her when he'd done quite the opposite. He'd healed her. She answered with a shake of the head. "No. That was wonderful. You are wonderful."

He looked down at her with eyes overflowing with love. "I loved making love with you. I want to do it again. And again after that."

She brought his face to hers and answered with a long, impassioned kiss. "Me too."

He stared at her for a long moment. So long that Delaney almost asked him if something was wrong. Finally he said, "That's good to hear. But it doesn't explain the faraway look in your eyes. You're somewhere else." He rolled off of her and covering them with a blanket, gathered her in his arms.

She molded herself into the crook of his shoulder as if second nature. "I'm here. It's just that…" She gulped and decided to go on. "It's never been like that for me before."

She felt his breath catch. Then he asked in a hopeful voice, "Because you haven't been with anyone for awhile?"

Delaney willed herself not to take the easy way out. "No, I don't think that's it. I—," she got out before Mike's phone began ringing. He didn't move a muscle. "Aren't you going to get that?"

"No."

"It might be important. Especially at this hour."

"Not as important as this. Besides, if it'll really important, they'll try again. You were saying?"

"I—," she repeated, as one of Springsteen's unmistakable guitar rifts filled the room again.

Mike let out an aggravated breath. "Hold that thought." He retrieved his jeans from the floor, then produced the phone with a grimace. "It's Brian... Hey...Oh, hi, Linds."

Delaney looked on as Mike's troubled expression gave way to a grin.

"Laney? Yeah, she got in fine." He listened, then went on in a voice higher than usual. "She hasn't answered her cell or at the house? Sure, I could go over there and check on her. But that's not necessary. She's right here." He paused for a few beats, as if letting the words sink in. "Do you want to talk to her?...Okay, here she is." Getting back in bed, he handed over the phone with a smirk.

Delaney shot him a look of amused mortification and cleared her throat. "Hey."

"Hey. I'm sorry to interrupt," Lindsay said hurriedly. "I wanted to make sure you got settled. I got concerned when you didn't answer either phone."=

"You're sweet to worry. My cell is in the other room. Thanks again. Your place is great."

"Of course."

There was a weighty lull, allowing Delaney to picture Lindsay biting her lip and pacing. Then she began again, "Laney, I—"

Delaney put her out of her misery. "I know. It's okay, I promise. How's Maui?" she asked, putting the matter to rest. "Have you even left the room?"

"Yes," Lindsay defended loftily. "We went out to dinner last night and took a sightseeing cruise today." She paused as if inwardly debating, then added, "I'll let you go. Can I talk to Mike again real quick?"

"Sure." Delaney gave Mike the phone. "She wants to talk to you again."

He took it with an irritated stare. "Yeah." After a few seconds, he sighed tiredly and excused himself. He was so tight and cut, Delaney thought as he walked naked across the room. She'd loved having him kneeling above her, drilling her so powerfully and muttering her name over and over. She'd forgotten what it felt like to be wanted. Or maybe she'd never known true want before.

Back turned to her, he leaned against the bathroom door frame with the phone to his ear. What could Lindsay have to talk to him about? Mike raised an impatient hand to his forehead and shifted to the right. Whatever it was, he didn't want to hear it. He had something else on his mind. His profile was proof of that.

"Okay. I stepped away. What's up?"

"I'm sorry if I interrupted something. And since I think I did, I don't have to tell you what an amazing person Delaney is."

"No, you don't."

"Part of what makes her so amazing is how resilient she is. Life has not been kind to her. Many people would have taken the easy road. Or just thrown in the towel. She didn't."

"I know. Neither did you. Or Brian. Or myself for that matter."

"Granted. But when Laney thought she was finally on steady ground, she was knocked down again. Hard. She could have gone on the rebound and settled for the first guy to come along. But she didn't."

"I'm well aware of that, Linds."

"Going out to dinner with you was an enormous step. Did she tell you she hasn't dated anyone in two years? Let alone..." Lindsay's voice trailed off.

Mike had had just about enough of this. "What are you getting at?"

"Be careful with her, Mike. Her heart was shattered. It may look like it's back together, but it's not. I was the same way until I realized that only Brian could make me whole again. It wasn't that easy for her. Ryan wasn't the answer."

"I hope to hell not," Mike grunted derisively. He raked this fingers through his hair and walked over to the bathroom mirror. He looked different somehow, in his eyes especially. "I'm not going to hurt her." He returned to the conversation. "I care about her."

"I know you wouldn't intentionally hurt her. But please, just be honest with her," Lindsay pleaded. "Ryan no doubt knew long before their wedding day it wasn't right. She already trusts you or she wouldn't have slept with you."

"Actually I think it has something to do with my telling her I've fallen in love with her."

There was a sharp intake of breath. "Mike."

"You heard me. I'm not him. I'm not going to hurt her. I want her. She wants me. We'll figure it out from there. She trusts me, so can you?"

"Yes, of course." Then voice cracking, she told him, "She's the second luckiest girl in San Francisco, Mike."

"Well, that makes me the second luckiest guy in San Francisco. Because apparently she's in love with me too. Now get back to your honeymoon. Everything is fine here," he assured her, catching another glimpse of his reflection. What was it? It was driving him crazy.

❧

"And I thought you couldn't be any more perfect."

Delaney sent Mike a perplexed look and cocked her head to one side.

"The magazine," he explained, sliding under the blanket. "You're a sports fan on top of being smart, beautiful and sexy?"

She'd been thumbing through the *Sports Illustrated* on the nightstand, trying to occupy her restless mind while Mike was speaking to Lindsay. "Growing up in Chicago, you can't help but be a sports fan," she replied. "Besides, it's still a man's world out there. I have to be able to hold my own." She tossed the magazine aside. "Everything okay in Maui?"

Mike eased her back on the bed. "Fine. Mrs. Rembrandt is playing mother hen, fretting about everybody else. You're the object of her concern du jour."

"Me?"

Nodding, he framed her head with his arms and elaborated, "She's afraid I'm going to hurt you." His expression fell. "Are you afraid of that too? Is that what you were starting to say?"

"No. I mean yes," she fumbled a bit. "But that's not what I was saying before."

He started kissing her neck. "What, then?"

Delaney shut her eyes and let her heart do the talking. "I've never felt that connected to a man before. It threw me a little."

Instantly Mike's mouth froze and his entire body stiffened. He stared at her blankly for a few seconds before turning his body away.

Delaney's stomach sank. What was she thinking, telling him that? The last thing she wanted was for him to feel trapped because they'd slept together. He'd had countless women in his bed, she reminded herself. And her rusty performance probably left much to be desired. Trembling inside, she sat up and scanned the room for her clothes. Her jeans were on the floor and she spotted her shirt off to the side, but her panties were nowhere to be seen. She would have to live without them. "I should go," she managed quietly, swinging her legs over the side of the bed.

"Go?" Mike snapped out of the trance. "Why do you want to go?" He grabbed her arm. "Do you need something from Brian's?"

"No." Oddly modest, she brought the blanket up to cover her breasts. "I don't know what Lindsay said to you, but I don't want you to feel obligated. I don't have to stay."

Mike sprung up. "What are you talking about?" He ran an unconscious hand through his hair. "I want you to stay tonight and tomorrow night and every night until you go home. I thought you wanted that too," he asked with eyes full of confusion.

The trepidation in the pit of her stomach eased a little. "I do. But you seemed distant all the sudden. I've never slept with a man I've only known for a week. Or fallen in love with him," she admitted shyly, looking down. "I don't know the protocol."

Mike lifted her chin. "Neither have I. The falling in love part, at least," he amended through a grin and folded her into his arms. "And I've never bonded with someone like that before either."

She clung to him for dear life as the tears she hadn't known she was shedding soaked the cuff of the blanket. "You haven't?"

"No." He exhaled deliberately. "Now, do you still want to leave?"

She shook her head from side to side. "I never wanted to leave. I thought you wanted me to."

"I didn't. I don't." He paused, then decided to go on. "That's what scares me. I don't think I'll ever want you to leave. But you will. Unless you want to stay." He eased her away just enough to dry her cheeks. "And that's even scarier. Because if we both feel that way already, it means something much more than great sex is happening here." He planted a kiss on her forehead, then lightened, "But to be sure, we should probably try it again."

Laughing a little, Delaney laid back and threw the blanket off invitingly. "Yeah, we probably should. To be sure."

He skimmed her face with his fingertips, as if seeing her for the first time. Then he feathered kisses down her throat to her breasts, tugging on one nipple, then the other. She beckoned him back to mouth where his lazy tongue met hers, then skimmed across her teeth, igniting a current that rumbled through her body and settled between her legs.

She took him in her hands and began to stroke him, slowly at first, then more urgently. His fingers found her again and he kept pace with her, and she grew as wet as he hard. Flames were engulfing her insides now and she wondered if she would explode from the want. She could feel the arch of gratification building and in reaching for it, quieted her busy hands. Still, Mike grew in them as the wave of pleasure hit and she crested. When she opened her eyes, he was beholding her in awe. "I love watching you. I love knowing I can do that to you." He scooted back and extended his hand. "Sit up. This time I don't want to miss a thing."

She rose to meet him and took hold of him again. He was oozing.

"See what you do to me? I loved being inside you. I can't wait to be inside you again."

She coiled her legs around him. "Then don't."

He slid into her with a long, throaty groan. Her breasts nestled against his chest, they began to climb to the summit together. Back and forth they swayed, then began to rock as the friction between them increased, accelerated. Until, as if scripted, Delaney threw her head back and howled just as Mike erupted into her and they reached that glorious peak of release together.

CHAPTER ELEVEN

"READY?" MIKE WALKED INTO Brian's apartment the next day.

"Almost," Delaney replied, securing an earring as she entered the kitchen.

She wore a cream-colored skirt and jacket with something silky underneath. Something he would look forward to removing later.

"You look great."

"Thanks. I'm a bit overdressed for the California office, but I have a business dinner tonight. I won't have time to change."

Mike didn't try to hide his disappointment. "Oh. I assumed we'd go out to dinner tonight, since I'm working the weekend."

"I'd much rather do that, but I don't think I can reschedule," she told him through a frown. "This was originally planned for Thursday evening, but Tom has a conflict."

Mike cleared his throat. "Tom?"

"Tom Langdon, my boss' counterpart here," she explained. "Intuition tells me this is an interview of sorts, in case she doesn't come back from maternity leave this time. Senior management from all the divisions weigh in when it comes to filling executive positions. Since I was in town we decided to meet for dinner."

Mike pushed away the unfamiliar, bothersome feeling in the pit of his stomach. "So you know him?"

Nodding, she flung her huge purse over her shoulder. It reminded Mike of how his stomach had jumped when he first saw her on the plane. "When I first started at Hudson and Grace, Tom worked in the Chicago office. He moved out here a few years ago to run the West Coast operation." She walked over to Mike and put her arms around his neck. "When I made this arrangement, I had no evening plans to consider. I didn't have anyone to have dinner with."

Mike relaxed a little. "Well, you do now," he told her with kiss. He'd just had her and all he could think about was having her again. He ran his hands up and down her back. "Will you be late?"

"I doubt it. We're meeting at six o'clock. Some Italian place in the Financial District," she answered with a dismissive shrug. "Speaking of which, if we're grabbing something to eat before I head in, we need to get going."

"Okay." Mike surveyed the living room as they broke apart. "Where's your suitcase? We can drop it off at my place on the way out. That way you won't have to run back and forth later."

She didn't answer immediately, instead met his expectant stare with a tentative one. After a few blinks she said, "It's in the bedroom. I'm not packed up, though. I wanted to make sure that was still what you wanted."

Her eyes were wide and rimmed in apprehension and she appeared to be holding her breath. Like he'd held his last night when she'd said she was leaving. "It's exactly what I want," he told her unequivocally. "That's not going to change. I want to fall asleep with you tonight and wake up with you tomorrow. And the next day. Got it?"

She affirmed with a nod and tears welling in her eyes as she fell back into his arms. Her breathing was shallow, like she was fighting to keep them at bay. He felt his mouth open, then close, biting off the words. Mike had never told a woman that he truly loved her before. Because he never had. For the first time in his life he felt real, raw love. The kind people kill for and die for and search their entire lives for. Once he told Delaney he loved her like that, there was no turning back. So he had to be sure. Sure enough for both of them.

◞

A dreary fog swaddled San Francisco in a misty, gray cloak as Delaney rounded the corner on California Avenue. Her afternoon in the office had been productive, considering her marketing plan had some hefty competition for her attention these days. She couldn't get Mike out of her mind, not that she wanted to. What she wanted was to push away the foreboding angst that lingered in her gut.

By the time she arrived at the restaurant, Tom was already seated with a glass of wine. "Sorry I'm late." Delaney returned the hospitable hug and slid into the leather booth across from her dinner companion. Tom was tall, broad and impossibly handsome. If it wasn't his wavy, jet-black hair or golden skin, it was his incredibly toned body. His looks were legendary at Hudson and Grace, a fact not lost on him. He had a decade on Delaney and as much as he loved women, had never been married. "I was on the phone with Alan," she explained. "He was on the way to his house in Michigan and had all the time in the world to chat."

Tom's chiseled face instantly became a disgusted scowl. "I guess when you're Senior VP, next in line for CEO, you can bail on Wednesday for the weekend."

"Midwestern summers are short compared to those in California. You have to take advantage of the warm weather while you can," Delaney reminded him. Apparently Tom still harbored some resentment about being passed over for the position. "I've been gone for a week and with Liz out, Alan has been in the trenches." She paused and gave the waitress her drink order, then finished, "A long weekend with his family will do him good."

"Whatever," Tom snickered with a dismissive shake of the head. "I've been in the trenches for twice as long as Alan. Literally. I started in the mailroom, remember?" His gaze shifted to the menu. "But that's neither here nor there. What do you feel like tonight? The Chicken Parm here is out of this world."

"I had a late lunch, so I'm not very hungry," Delaney replied, skimming the menu. "Maybe just a salad."

She felt Tom's appraising stare for a long moment. Then he cleared his throat and said, "Whatever you decide, save room for dessert. I want to take you to this coffeehouse in North Beach. They make the most incredible cannoli," he elaborated. "They open for breakfast, then close again until evening to serve the after dinner crowd. Unique business model. I wish I'd thought of it."

Delaney stared blankly at her menu, not absorbing a word after *I want to take you*. There was something different about the tone of his voice, the cadence of his words all of the sudden. It was familiar, intimate, decisive. Like this was a dinner date instead of a business dinner. "Thanks anyway, but I'm not up for a late night," she declined nonchalantly. "Besides having my presentation in the morning, I'm still recovering from my whirlwind weekend in Tahoe." And Mike was at home waiting for her.

"I hope you'll reconsider." Undaunted, Tom forged on. "I've been looking forward to it. How was Tahoe anyway? You were up there for a wedding, right?"

Just then the waitress returned. She served the wine and took their dinner order. After she walked away, Delaney replied, "Right. I'd forgotten how beautiful it was."

"You can't be beat Tahoe this time of year. I've been trying to carve out a weekend to go up for some R&R. Hate to go alone, though," he finished with a loaded stare.

Fidgeting in her seat, Delaney changed the subject. "I can't get over the office atmosphere here. It's much more relaxed than Chicago. The place was a ghost town before six."

"We Californians take quitting time seriously. Speaking of which, word has it Liz isn't returning in the fall. You've got your ear to the ground at corporate. What's your take on it?"

More relaxed now that they were back to discussing business, Delaney told him, "Liz was planning to take three months off, which will likely turn into six now. She was already struggling with an executive workload and motherhood. And with the baby being premature, her day care options are more limited. It's barbaric that women still feel that they have to choose between career and family," she continued. "As a company, we need to do more to find a middle ground. Liz is an intricate part of our team. Her departure would leave quite a void."

Tom cocked his head to the side and took a liberal sip of wine. "I agree, but no one is irreplaceable. You should know your name is on the short list if Liz resigns. You have my full endorsement. She would no doubt feel the same way."

Delaney didn't attempt to conceal the grin spreading across her face. "That means a great deal to me. Thank you for your support. I would embrace the opportunity should it arise."

"I'm sure." He leaned forward and covered Delaney's hand with his. Then, his cornflower blue eyes clinging to hers, said, "But that's only part of the reason I invited you to dinner."

Delaney's stomach plunged, taking the grin with it. "Oh?"

Tom flashed his infamous toothy smile. "I've been interested in seeing you socially for some time. I know you were dealing with some personal issues. I hope that's behind you. I'd love to take you out for a romantic dinner, maybe a show while you're in town." He finished assuredly, "What night works best for you?"

He'd come by his confidence honestly, she supposed. He'd probably never been turned down for a date. Or anything else. That was about to change. Delaney cleared her throat and chose her words carefully. "Tom, I'm incredibly flattered. But I'm seeing someone." She heard herself say, her tone a mix of sincerity and revelation.

"You are?" he marveled. Then in response to Delaney's arched eyebrows, quickly qualified. "I mean, I didn't realize that. Is the relationship serious? Monogamous?"

That was an excellent question, Delaney thought, as the knots in her stomach wound tighter. Outside of Mike's conversation with Jessica, they really hadn't defined their relationship. And in a few days, in addition to being presumably monogamous and serious, it would also be long-distance.

"I'm not asking for exclusivity here," Tom was still talking. "I've always thought there was a spark between us. I'd like to explore it."

If she hadn't met Mike, would she have accepted? No, she told herself. Tom and his ego did nothing for her. "Yes, it's monogamous and serious," she confirmed. "But even if it wasn't, I don't think it would be a good idea for us to see each other socially. Especially with the VP position potentially on the table."

Tom waved away the argument. "Don't worry about that. If you get the job, everyone knows it would be on merit. You've more than earned it."

She had indeed, Delaney reminded herself with a mental kick. And Mike was making her realize how much she'd sacrificed to get where she was. Maybe that had added to Ryan's disillusion with her. She wouldn't make that mistake again.

Just then their dinners arrived. They ate and conversed easily, trading office gossip and sharing rumors of impending promotions and organizational shake-ups. By the time the waitress returned, Delaney felt more relaxed.

"Can I interest you in coffee or dessert?"

"No," Tom declined, tossing a knowing look Delaney's way. "I think the lady has other plans. I'll take the check."

"Of course, Mr. Langdon," she said, reaching into her front pocket and handing him a leather folder.

Delaney watched the other woman walk away. Then she said, "Thank you for dinner, Tom."

He scribbled his name. "My pleasure." Standing, he stated in a diplomatic voice, "You're staying at the Fairmont, right? I'll see you back."

"That's okay," she told him hurriedly. "I'll be fine."

"I insist." He extended his arm, inviting her to walk ahead of him.

The night air bit her face as they exited the restaurant and turned north on Mason. It was easier to let him walk her to the Fairmont than explain she was no longer staying there, Delaney decided on the fly.

After a few silent paces he inquired, "So who is he? Anyone I know?"

"I doubt it." She hesitated, then supplied, "He's a pilot."

"No wonder you've been traveling so much," he said with a chuckle. "Is that how you met him? On a flight?"

"Kind of. We have a mutual friend," she explained, hoping that would satisfy his curiosity.

Tom put his hands in the pockets of his deeply creased pants. "Well, I hope he knows how lucky he is."

Stunned and touched, Delaney turned to face him. "What a nice thing to say."

He returned the smile and they walked along companionably as the cable cars clanged merrily through the soupy air. When they reached the hotel, Tom stopped just outside of the revolving door.

"Thanks for walking me back."

"Of course. I won't wish you good luck for tomorrow; you won't need it. I'm sorry I can't be there." He started to walk away, then stopped short. When he turned back around, his expression was unusually humble. "Do me a favor. Let me know if it doesn't work out."

"I will," Delaney promised with a smile. She walked into the lobby and waited until he was out of sight before heading back the way they'd come. She drew her jacket around her, and despite the bone-chilling air, wished it was a longer walk to Mike's apartment. Tom's proposition had forced her to face a reality she could no longer avoid. Committing to a long-distance relationship with someone you'd only known for a week was a lot to ask. But she couldn't have it any other way. By the time she arrived at Mike's building, the knots in her stomach had turned into spikes. Hands shaking, she ran the security card Lindsay had given her through the reader. The lock released and she stepped into the waiting elevator. She leaned against the mirrored walls with a sigh as the car sped to the top floor. Despite remembering the code, she raised her hand and knocked.

Within seconds Mike greeted her with a warm smile. "Why didn't you let yourself in?" He stepped aside to let her enter, then closed the door and took her in his arms. "I was just about to call you. Did you take a cab home?"

Delaney didn't answer, just fell into him and rested her head on his shoulder. She could feel his heart begin to canter, chasing hers. He kissed her hair and pulled back just enough to meet her eyes. His smile quickly faded. "Are you okay? Didn't it go well?"

She ran her forefingers under her damp bottom lashes. "It was fine. Tom is completely supportive of me in that role."

Mike gave her a puzzled look, then ushered her over to the couch. He dropped his arm around her shoulders and drew her close. "Then why the tears?"

She let out a shallow breath and digging deep said, "Tom was interested in more than dinner."

Mike stiffened. "Oh? How so?"

"He wanted to see me again while I was in town. Socially," she dragged out the word.

He nodded markedly, then asked, "What did you say?"

"I said no, of course. I don't think it's a good idea to mix business with pleasure."

"Of course," Mike agreed in a clipped voice. "So you're upset because his romantic interest in you cheapens his professional endorsement?"

"No, I have that either way."

"Then what's the problem?"

Delaney saw the dejected look in his eyes and knew he felt as she did. The dread in the pit of her stomach turned to joy and she felt the corners of her mouth curve. "There isn't one. I wasn't sure until just now. I told him I was in a relationship. A serious, monogamous relationship. That I had no—"

Mike's mouth pouncing on hers prevented her from finishing the sentence. He kissed her so affectingly that the tears returned, this time rolling down her cheeks. "Laney, you scared the hell out of me," he admitted, eyes darting back and forth furiously.

Her heart leapt to her throat. "Am I right? Am I in a serious, monogamous relationship with the man I've fallen so deeply in love with?"

"Do you want to be?"

Shallowing hard, Delaney nodded.

"Then you are." Then forehead crinkling, he asked, "Did he make a pass at you?"

"No." She shook her head. "Tom is nothing if not a gentleman. He's also successful, attractive and intelligent. He was quite taken aback. He's not used to rejection."

"Well, he'd better get used to it where you're concerned. You're officially off the market. "Providing I'm the man you've fallen in love with, that is."

She shot him a wise look. "What do you think?"

"I think I want to consummate our serious, monogamous relationship. Right here, right now."

"I think we've already done that," she told him playfully. "Several times."

"That was before. Everything is different now. Because now I know you're mine."

Wooed by Mike's words, Delaney went for broke. "I've been yours since I saw you on the plane. That's when I first fell in love with you."

"Laney..." He searched her eyes. Then he kissed her tenderly, as if she would break. "I feel like I fall in love with you over and over again."

She didn't return the words, but instead shed her jacket and skirt and slid her shirt over her head. Then she threw her bra aside and reclining back on the cool leather, extended her arms in invitation.

His eyes fired with lust as he grazed the palms of his hands over her breasts, then removed his clothes and covered her body with his. She arched in welcome as he began kissing her neck, moaned as he caressed her nipples until they stood on point, and quivered in anticipation as he shimmied her out of her panties. Wrapping her hand around his erection, she grated him against her, then slid him into her wetness. He uttered affirmations and gratifications as she guided him deeper into her. Their shared moans filled the steamy air between their bodies as he began to move inside her. Giving her all of him, sending her on a journey of need until she felt the heady spasms build and the sweet heat of ecstasy consume her. Then wanting the same for him, she bent her knees and lifted her buttocks, bringing him deeper still. They rocked together heedlessly, recklessly, until he drained himself into her, staking his claim.

∾

"Did you find her?" the caller demanded without preamble.

"Not yet. Still chasing pavement."

"I'm not paying you to chase pavement. Richards got released early. If I didn't have his P.O. in my pocket, you'd be looking for him too."

Watson twirled a toothpick between his teeth, wishing it was a cigarette. Like that was his fault. "I can grab her at the airport if nothing else. Her outbound arrangements haven't changed."

"By then Richards could be in the wind. Along with my money. And yours."

"That wasn't the deal. I found the girl."

"The deal was to get to Richards. How you went about making that happen was on you."

Watson let his mouth get ahead of his brain. "For all you know the money's gone. Or he never had it to begin with."

"He's got it. He's just too smart to brag about it." The other man stepped up his already contemptuous tone. "Find her before I find you."

Watson contemplated the portentous vacuum of disconnection for a moment. He had to get his head on straight. Besides getting him nowhere, the swanky people going in and out of the Fairmont only reminded him that he stuck out like a sore thumb around here. Raising his collar to combat the dank night air, he turned east and disappeared into the shadows.

CHAPTER TWELVE

"THINGS SURE HAVE CHANGED," Mike told Delaney a day later, navigating them through a throng of black and orange. "I remember going to Candlestick as a kid and not even waiting in line."

"I'm sure Barry Bonds breaking Hank Aaron's home run record here didn't hurt attendance."

Mike fell a little deeper in love. "Good memory for a Cubs fan."

"My grandfather was a huge baseball fan." She glanced at him over the rim of her sunglasses. "And the Giants come east a couple of times a year, you know."

"Okay, Miss Smarty Pants. Who threw the pitch to Bonds that night?"

She considered for a moment, then tipped her chin. "Bacsik. From the Nationals."

Mike sent her a look of shocked reverence.

"I have to have something to talk about at those boring business dinners," she explained dryly.

They weaved through the packed atrium hand in hand. Mike was directing Delaney toward the elevators at the Second Street gate when a thought suddenly struck him.

"Have you ever been to a Giant's home game before?"

"No."

"So you've never had the ballpark garlic fries?"

She shook her head from side to side. "Are they as good as everyone says?"

"Better." He turned on his heel.

"Where are we going?"

"To buy tickets."

She frowned. "I thought you had season tickets."

"I do. Box seats behind the dugout."

"Then why are we buying tickets?"

"Because the best way to experience your first Giants game isn't in a box. It's in the stands."

Mike stopped in front of the ticket window and reached into his back pocket. "Two. View Level." He finished the transaction, then turned to Delaney. "It can get pretty cold up there after the sun goes down. Do you want to get another sweatshirt?"

"I'll be fine in this one of yours. I'm a Chicago girl, remember?"

He did. Unfortunately.

Fifteen minutes later they were in their seats high above home plate. "Look at the bay."

Delaney commented, wide-eyed. "The way it sparkles in the sunshine. The cars look like ants inching across the bridge."

Mike had seen the bay, the bridge, the hills, thousands of times, but seeing it with her made him feel like it was the first time. Like everything else. He indulged himself in her for a few seconds, then told her, "Enjoy it while you can. The fog could roll in at any minute."

She smiled up at him, then snuggled so close Mike could smell the shampoo in her hair. His shampoo. From his shower.

They watched the Giants fend off the Padres for a few innings. Then he asked, "Are you ready for those garlic fries? I could use another Coke."

"Sure."

He straightened up, easing her away in the process. "There's a Gilroy's on this level. I'll get us a couple of hot dogs too."

"Want me to go with you?"

"No, watch the game. I'll be right back."

Mike made quick work of the steps, following the scent of garlic wafting through the heavy air. The line was six people deep and three across. He was standing there, finishing his drink when he realized the man to his right was talking to him.

"Packed for a Thursday night, huh?"

Mike gave him a perfunctory smile. "Yeah. First home game since the All-Star Break."

"Think we're gonna pull it out?"

Before he could answer, a gruff voice behind him said, "Go ahead."

With a jolt, Mike stepped forward and placed his order. "Sorry," he threw over his shoulder.

"No problem." The man was swarthy, with a deeply lined face and a crooked, cigarette-stained smile.

By the time Mike made it back to Delaney, the sun was setting behind the Oakland Hills, bouncing

off the water like a ball of copper. He handed her the food, then took his seat. "I didn't dare get us an order to share." He watched her pick up a fry and taste it, then reach for another. "What do you think?"=
"Hmm...worth the wait," she answered indulgently.

Mike, beholding her, couldn't agree more.

⁓

Colton checked the bands across his stomach one more time, then swung the duffle bag over his shoulder. Thanks to the thick athletic socks, no one would hear the rustling of the bills on his ankles. He had to laugh at the irony. Returning money was a helluva lot harder than stealing it.

He wiped the back of his hand across his brow. He was dripping with cold sweat. He didn't think it was possible to sleep in a less comfortable bed than his bunk in the hoosegow, but this one was killing his neck, he decided, directing his hand to the base of his skull.

There was no way he could get on a plane in a getup like this. He couldn't rent a car without a valid driver's license. Greyhound had been his only choice. There was still the matter of getting to the bus station without being jumped. Not surprisingly, the halfway house wasn't located in the best part of town. But if he could get through what lies between the two without incident, he'd be on his way to righting his second wrong.

CHAPTER THIRTEEN

"DO YOU WANT A glass of wine before we—" Walking into the bedroom the next night, Mike stopped short.

Delaney turned to him with a dubious shrug. "Well?"

The gown was full-length, like the one she'd worn to the wedding, but not cut as straight. Her hair fell to her bare shoulders in soft curls, shining as radiantly as the white stones adorning her neck. Her eyes looked darker, more mysterious than usual, behind thick lashes and liner.

She didn't wait for him to answer. Instead she returned to her reflection, bargaining, "I've never bought a red dress before, but I thought it would pop against my tan. Do you think the satin is too much?"

Mike shook off the stupor, but his erection was not so easily dismissed. "I think it's perfect. Effortlessly elegant just like you." He wrapped his arms around her waist and rested his chin on her shoulder. "But I'd still prefer it on the floor." He began kissing her throat, commending himself for rearranging his schedule for the weekend.

"Hmm." She tilted her head back with a contented sigh. "That can be arranged. But later."

She spun around and wreathed his neck. "You clean up pretty well yourself."

"It was about time I dusted off my tux." He let out a short breath and debated her slightly parted, glossy lips for a long moment. Then he brushed his against them saying, "But as beautiful as you look, there is one thing I would change."

Her expression fell a little. "It's my hair, isn't it? I was thinking about putting it up." She twisted the teeming locks up behind her head. "It's more sophisticated that way, like the dress. But leaving it down softens the neckline."

Mike had to laugh at the innocence in her voice. "I love your hair up or down, but the more I see of it the better. So I vote for down."

"Then down it is," she told him, smoothing the cuticle with her hands as her eyes filled with confusion. "What then?"

Reaching behind her neck, he unclasped the rhinestone necklace. "This." He reached into his jacket pocket. "I hope you'll agree."

She narrowed her eyes in confusion, then shifted them to the velvet box in his hand. "Mike, what is this?"

"Open it and find out," he challenged, placing it in her palm.

Her hands began to shake as she untied the silver ribbon and lifted the lid. "Mike," she gasped. "What have you done?"

"I bought you a present. Do you like it?" he asked, collecting the braid of rubies from their satin bed. "Damnedest thing. I had no idea your dress was red." He secured the clasp at the nape of her neck and took two steps back. The jewels sparkled like hundreds of bulbs on a Christmas tree. "There. Perfect."

He watched her forefinger find the teardrop pendant, then massage it. Gape-mouthed, she returned to the mirror. "Mike, it's absolutely beautiful."

"Not nearly as beautiful as you are." He handed her the matching earrings, also trimmed in diamonds. "I'll let you do this part. How you guys take those things in and out is beyond me."

She obliged, then studying her reflection, marveled, "I don't know what to say. It's incredible. But I can't accept it."

"Of course you can," he protested matter-of-factly. "I would be terribly offended otherwise."

She turned to face him. "You didn't have to do this."

He pressed a finger to her lips. "I know I didn't have to. I wanted to." He brushed away the wisps of hair falling into her face and wondered if she could feel just how much. "It's not something I do every day, you know. In fact, I've never done it before. And I hope it's the only the beginning."

Her eyes misted over and she threw her arms around him. "I hope so too. I mean only the

131

beginning of us," she clarified quickly, "not the jewelry."

He wondered if she had any idea how her words struck him. "Good. Now, are you almost ready? I'll never hear the end of it if we miss the meet and greet portion of the evening." He made air quotes with his fingers. "My son, the pilot."

"I'm ready," she told him, dabbing the corners of her eyes. "Thank you, by the way. I don't think I ever thanked you."

"The look on your face is almost thanks enough."

"Almost?"

"Yeah," he explained facetiously. "You can settle the balance later."

❧

The Fairmont Hotel towered into the night, drenching Nob Hill in warm, golden light. What a difference a week makes, Delaney thought as she stepped out of the car. Her life had done a three-sixty since the last time she was here.

"Good evening, folks. Welcome to the Fairmont. Will you be checking in or just spending the evening with us?"

"Just the evening, Charlie." Mike read the valet's gold name badge, then discretely slipped a bill into the older man's palm. "We're attending The Entrepreneurs Charity Ball."

"Thank you, sir," Charlie said, exchanging the bill for a numbered ticket. "You'll be epicureans in The Crown Room tonight. Best view in town."

"And so named," Mike added.

He nodded agreeably, then addressed Delaney. "Nice to see you again, Miss."

She returned the smile. "How sweet of you to remember."

"Couldn't forget a face as pretty as yours. Besides, someone was here the other day looking for you."

Delaney was stunned. "Me?"

"Had a picture of you and everything," Charlie went on nonchalantly. "But you'd already checked out by the time he caught up with you."

Mike and Delaney exchanged a baffled look. "Are you sure?"

"Positive," Charlie told her. "Short guy, mid-fifties, dark complexion."

She looked ahead unseeingly, unable to imagine who that could be, as that increasingly familiar sinking feeling began usurping her stomach.

"Ring any bells?" Mike was saying.

"None," Delaney told him. "No one outside of the office and you and Lindsay knew I was staying here."

"It sounded like this fellow expected you to still be here, like you'd changed your plans at the last minute. Unless he assumed you were staying here since you're attending the gala tonight," Charlie conjectured with a shrug.

"But I didn't even know I was going to be here tonight until yesterday."

"No, but you were supposed to be staying here through the weekend," Mike pointed out. "His information was correct, just not current." Reaching into his pant pocket, he retrieved his wallet. "Give me a call if he comes by again," he instructed Charlie. "But don't mention seeing us."

Charlie looked at the business card, then shifted his gaze back to Mike. "No problem. And no incentive necessary." He returned the second folded bill. "I had a bad feeling about that guy. He smelled fishy to me."

The men exchanged a look of unspoken understanding. Then Mike thanked Charlie and guided Delaney through the lobby. When they got into the elevator, she asked, "What do you think that was all about?"

"Probably nothing," Mike replied inadequately. "Let's not let it spoil our evening."

There was little opportunity for debate because only moments later the elevator doors opened and Delaney found herself on the top of the world. As if the bronze marble walls, gold coffered ceilings and candelabra chandeliers weren't enough, the ceiling-to-floor windows gave way to the most spectacular view of San Francisco Delaney had ever seen. The Golden Gate Bridge held court to the west, its orange trusses steeped against the inky sky. Next came Coit Tower, cradled by the mountains at its back and the city at its feet. Then the Bay Bridge, strung across the water like a beacon in the night, lit by the hundreds of cars snaking across its decks.

"Breathtaking, isn't it?" Mike read Delaney's mind. "I've lived in San Francisco for my entire life and nowhere else comes close on a clear night."

"Yeah," Delaney whispered in awe, taking in the room. "Are those balcony doors real? Can we go outside?"

"Not from this floor," Mike informed her. "You'll have to enjoy the view from behind the glass."

Just then a beckoning voice came from behind. "Michael, there you are." A woman with short platinum hair was approaching them with open arms. "I'm so glad you could make it after all."

"We just got here." Mike greeted her with a warm embrace. When he broke away, he returned to Delaney and circled her waist with his arm. "Mom, this is Delaney Richards. Laney, my mother, Patricia Savoy."

She gave Delaney a hospitable smile and extended her hand. "Lovely to meet you, Delaney. Welcome."

"Likewise. Thank you for having me, Mrs. Savoy."

Her amber eyes softened, accentuating the life lines framing them. "Tricia. And you can thank

Michael," she corrected gently. "He made quite a generous donation. This year we've adopted a homeless shelter for single mothers in Bernal Heights. We're hoping to raise enough money to build and furnish a twenty-bed addition."

"That's a cause close to my heart. I would be glad to make a donation of my own," Delaney offered.

Surprise and admiration rolled across Tricia's face. "That would be wonderful. Thank you," she said, sending Mike an affirming look.

"Well, well, who do we have here?" asked the man taking Mike into a half-hug.

"Dad, this is Delaney Richards. Laney my father—"

"Mike Savoy," the older version of Mike interrupted, kissing the top of Delaney's hand. "It's a pleasure to make the acquaintance of the second most beautiful woman in the room."

Delaney tried to return the positively captivating smile. "Thank you."

"Honestly, Mike," his wife mocked annoyance. "You say that to every woman you meet."

"But this time I really mean it." He shifted his gazed back to his son. "Michael, where are your manners? Your date is empty-handed." He signaled to a passing waiter, then addressed Delaney, "What's your poison?"

"A glass of red wine, please."

The waiter nodded in acknowledgement, then turned to Mike. "And you, sir?"

"Stella."

"Very well. Mrs. Savoy?"

"Nothing for me, thanks. I've got to get back to mingling. I see that the Mayor has just arrived." She turned to her husband. "Shall we?"

"I suppose we must," he sighed submissively. "We'll catch up with you two later."

Delaney watched them walk away, arms circling each other's waists inveterately.

"I know, I know, they're darling," Mike commented after a few seconds.

She threw him a clever look. "How did you know I was going to say that?"

"Because everybody says that."

"So they're always that way?"

"Pretty much," he told her with a shrug. "Occasionally they have words, but they always settle it in bed. Or so I'm told."

"How wonderful." Delaney felt her eyes welled up. "To love someone like that for fifty years."

"Yeah," Mike said, bringing her to him. "They found each other when they were young. And it lasted. Got lucky, I guess." He started to say something else, but swallowed it and pressed his lips to hers instead.

"Picture, folks?" asked a hopeful voice.

Mike turned to the man over his right shoulder. "Sure."

The photographer took three steps backward and lifted the camera from the lanyard around his neck. "On three. One, two, three." The camera rapid-fired several times, briefly illuminating the softy lit room. Then he stepped out from behind it and handed Mike a card. "I'll upload these tonight. They'll be available for thirty days," he informed them. "I also freelance for *The Chronicle*. I wouldn't be surprised if they picked one of these up. You two make a striking couple. Very photogenic." He thanked them and walked away.

Evocative silence hung over them for a long moment, then Mike suggested, "We should probably find our table and the rest of my family."

Delaney's stomach began to churn. "Okay."

He took her hand and led her through the maze of people, stopping occasionally for a quick handshake or a brief introduction. Finally they made it to the adjoining dining room. Mike paused and scanned the room, until his gaze rested on a woman waving to him from the far corner. "There they are," he announced and started walking again.

The fair-haired woman stood up from behind a round table surrounded by Chiavari chairs. Her gaze shifted from Mike to Delaney and grin growing, she touched the shoulder of the woman sitting next to her, directing her attention toward them.

Reading her mind, Mike squeezed Delaney's hand. "Don't worry, they don't bite. Not too hard anyway." After exchanging heartfelt hugs, Mike introduced Delaney to his sisters.

The fair-haired woman spoke first. "I'm Kathy."

"And I'm Jodi, Mike's Irish twin." Then in response to Delaney's puzzled squint, explained, "We're thirteen months apart."

"Oh," Delaney said, "of course."

"Come sit," Jodi invited, gesturing accordingly.

"Where are Brent and Joe?" Mike asked, pulling out Delaney's chair and taking the seat next to her.

"Downstairs getting another beer," Kathy answered. "The bar up here is closed until after dinner. God forbid they drink wine like the rest of us." Nodding to the open bottle in the center of the table, she rolled her eyes.

Mike's brothers-in-law returned and his older two sisters and their husbands arrived shortly thereafter. They all talked and ate companionably and by the time dessert was served, Delaney felt oddly at ease. So much so that when Jodi and Kathy announced they were going to the ladies room, she decided to join them.

"Bring her right back," Mike ordered with a suspicious look.

"Oh, we will." Kathy's hazel eyes twinkled facetiously. "After we set her straight on a few things."

Delaney started to get up, but Mike caught her arm. "Don't believe a word they say. They're evil."

"They don't look evil," she objected lightheartedly. "I think they're both quite beautiful."

"Seriously, come right back." He leaned in and brushed her lips. "I want to get out of here. I'm seeping just thinking about what you're wearing under that dress."

She shot him a look from under her lashes, then whispered in his ear, "What makes you think I'm wearing anything?"

His eyes fired with lust and he tried to pull her back to him, but she shook him off and followed the sisters into the hallway.

"Your necklace is gorgeous," Jodi complimented as they walked down the corridor, decorated in the same Venetian-style decor as the ballroom. "Did you have it designed just for that dress?"

"Oh, no. It was a gift." She hesitated, then added, "From Mike."

Both women instantly deadpanned her and Delaney wasn't sure if their subsequent halt was because they'd reached the lounge or that they found her words so shocking.

After a few silent beats, Kathy astonished, "Our brother, Mike?"

"Yeah." Delaney laughed a little, secretly pleased at their surprise. "I didn't want to accept it, but he insisted."

They exchanged a baffled look, then asked concertedly, "Why wouldn't you accept it?"

Delaney let out a shallow breath. "We haven't known each other for very long. To be honest, I felt a bit odd about coming tonight. I didn't want to impose."

After another shared glance, Jodi remarked in earnest, "I hope we didn't make you feel that way."

"Oh, no! Not at all," Delaney told them hurriedly and meant it. "It's just that…" She searched the geometric-patterned carpeting for the words. "I know there have been many women in Mike's life. You probably tire of making small talk with all of them."

Jodi shot her sister a knowing look and placed the palms of her hands on Delaney's forearms. "There might be many women in Michael's life, but we haven't met any of them. She wouldn't admit it, but sometimes I think Mom wonders about him. Having four sisters and all." She smiled without parting her lips and her soft brown eyes hinted at tears. "So you must be very special to him. Or you wouldn't be here."

Her kind words rendered Delaney speechless, but she managed a grateful smile. She was standing in front of the lounge mirror brushing her hair with them a few minutes later, wondering when this fairy tale would end, when the swish of the door drew their collective attention.

"Here you all are," Tricia announced grandly. "Is everybody all right? Michael is outside pacing like an expectant father."

Kathy spoke first. "We're fine." She waved her mother over. "Come see the necklace Michael gave to Delaney."

Delaney's stomach fell to her toes as Tricia approached her. For all this woman knew, she was a gold digger. Or worse, the kind of woman who would accept expensive jewelry from a man she'd only known for a week in exchange for other things.

After a short contemplation, Tricia asked, "May I?"

"Of course," Delaney replied, feeling fever rush to her cheeks.

Tricia brushed her fingertips across the pendant, then held it between her thumb and forefinger. "It's positively stunning. Although anything would be on you, dear," she remarked, shifting her gaze upward. "Earrings too; I trained him well." Then as if struck by a weighty realization, she took a marked step back. Her eyes misted with tears, but she quickly blinked them away. "I must say, he comes by his good taste honestly. His father is never one to disappoint."

"I don't think Michael's ever done anything like that before. Has he, Mom?."

"No, Katherine. Not that I know of." Tricia's voice was flat.

"He rarely brings a date to anything, let alone buy her jewelry," Jodi chimed in.

"You're right, girls." Tricia's eyes found Delaney's again and held. "Which means Delaney must be much more than a date."

CHAPTER FOURTEEN

"WHAT WERE YOU GUYS doing in there for so long?" Mike asked Delaney a few minutes later after exchanging parting pleasantries with his family.

"Freshening up, talking." Her tone was elusive.

Mike had heard the term "freshening up" for as long as he could remember and still had no idea what it meant. "What were you talking about?"

"This and that," she replied coyly. "They were filling my head with all kinds of stories about you."

"All lies, no doubt."

"I hope not." Humor flashed into her eyes. "Michael."

"Very funny," he told her, sliding his hand into hers as the elevator beeped, then stopped.

"That was quick," Delaney commented as the doors opened. She started to take a step forward, then stopped short. "Oh! No wonder. This isn't the lobby."

"No, it's not."

Her eyes narrowed in confusion as he led her out into the hall. "Then why are we getting off?"

"You'll see." Slowing their pace and retrieving a key card from his pocket, he slid it through the reader. "After you," he directed, gesturing for her to enter.

He watched her eyes sweep the repetitive-hued suite, then the terrace. The double doors were open, allowing the breeze to raise the curtains puddling on the floor. Beyond, the silhouette of the city was framed in black filigree.

"You wanted a balcony," he reminded her mildly.

She turned to him in open-mouthed wonder, then walked through the living room and out onto the terrace. Her fingertips brushed the back of the cushions on the wrought iron chairs as she made her way to the railing. "I don't know what to say."

He followed her. "Say you'll stay here with me tonight."

She studied him in bewilderment, as if the question was absurd. "Of course I'll stay here with you. I'll go anywhere with you."

Because she loved and trusted him, he inwardly amazed. He brought her hands to his lips and kissed them. "I know how hard it is for you to trust someone again. I won't let you down, I promise." He hesitated, then decided the time had come. "I love you so much, Laney."

He watched her eyes fill and mouth tighten as she bit back the tears. Then she declared with a catch in her voice, "I love you, too. So much. And I'm so scared."

Mike let out an overdue breath. "So am I. I've never really loved anyone before."

"Neither have I."

He jolted back a little, nonplussed. "But you were engaged."

She shook her head from side to side. "That wasn't real love. I know that now. That part of me didn't exist before you." She fell into him and the tears sprung from her eyes, sprinkling the collar of his white shirt in black spots.

Looking upward, he gave silent thanks. Then he said, "And as if that isn't enough, my family loved you too."

He felt her release a sigh of relief. "They did?"

"Yes, of course. Why wouldn't they?"

"For one thing, I was worried about being compared to the other women in your life."

"That's impossible. There's no one for them to compare you to. Not that they would anyway. My family isn't like—"

"I don't mean that way," Delaney demurred.

"Let me finish, please." Suddenly agitated, he raked a hand through his hair and began to pace on the terrace. "There is no one for them to compare you to because I've never introduced them to someone like you before. Occasionally I've brought a woman, a date, a friend, to family gatherings, but never the same woman twice. Sometimes we wouldn't even stay the evening, let alone," he glanced at his watch and confirmed his suspicion, "until midnight."

She started to say something, but he halted her with his palm. "You're right. There have been many women in my life, in my bed. Very few of whom have met my family. None of whom I've given jewelry to, missed when we're apart for a few hours, thought about constantly, rearranged my schedule for." He returned to her. "And most importantly, loved."

Her eyes were shining, dancing now. "You rearranged your schedule?"

Mike was beside himself. "Out of all that, the schedule part is was what you got?"

"No. I got the loved part at the end."

"Laney," he whispered with jagged breath. "Of course they loved you. I knew they would. What's not to love?"

She laughed away the words. "Oh, I can think of a few things."

"I can only think of one."

Dismay replaced the goodwill in her eyes and her brows knotted. "You can?"

"Yeah," he declared evenly. "Loving each other isn't enough for me."

He watched the color drain from her face. "It's not?"

"No." He raised their joined hands. "I want you to belong to me. I want to belong to you too."

"I do." She tripped over the words. "I thought you already did."

"I mean for good." He stoked her cheek with the back of his fingers, knowing he'd been sure all along. "I mean forever. Can you see yourself loving me forever?"

She smiled and with a measured nod managed, "Can you see yourself loving me forever?"

"I know I can. I know I want to. I want to make love to you tonight and every night for the rest of my life. You and only you."

She seemed to truly believe him for the first time. "I want that too," she assured him in a voice filled with deep emotion. "I could never be with another man now. I couldn't bear for you to touch someone else."

"I won't," he promised, cradling her chin in his hands. "Ever. I'm not asking you tonight. I won't rush you. I just needed to know if—"

She quieted his lips with her forefinger. "The answer is yes. Whether you ask me tonight or a thousand nights from now."

Indescribably happy, Mike tasted her tears, then rested his forehead against hers. "That will have to wait until I can ask you properly. However," his mouth found hers again and began to feed, "there is something I can ask you tonight."

She tilted her head back as he showered her throat with kisses. "Hmm. What would that be?"

"I want to taste you. I want you to taste me too."

That seemed to surprise, then entice her. She righted her head and found his gaze with wide eyes. "You can do anything you want to me." Her tone was dark and full of challenge. "I'm yours, remember?"

He could do nothing but mumble her name, willing his moral compass to hold steady.

But her ensuing words made that nearly impossible. "You'll be the first man to touch me that way. Now I wish you were the only man to ever touch me at all."

Mike swallowed the shock and wondered if she could feel him hardening behind the zipper. "As long as I'm the last."

She responded by silently backing up into the bedroom and reaching behind her. A second later the dress fell to the floor, leaving her naked. "I've been waiting all night to show you what's under my dress."

He supposed the foghorns still bellowed from the bridges, the seals continued to bark on the pier, the cars buzzed along on the street below, but Mike's mind discounted all that. In his head, his hands were already running down Delaney's shoulders, lingering at the curve of her breasts before pausing on her waist and then resting on her hips. He shut the French doors behind him and loosened his collar. "I've been waiting all night to see what's under that dress."

"I told you," she licked her lips. "Didn't you believe me?"

He cast aside his suit coat. "Oh, I believed you. That's what I've been waiting all night for."

By mid-stride, he felt himself being yanked under her spell. By the time he reached her, his hands felt clumsy against the buttons of his shirt. Hers, on the other hand, were as agile as a cat. "You seemed oddly patient." She ran her fingers down the shirt, unbuttoning it slowly, holding him with a wolfish smile all the while. "I was beginning to wonder."

"You'll never have to wonder about that." Tipping point reached and passed, he grabbed her wrists. "If I'd had my way, I would've taken you in the elevator." He ripped the shirt off before she could finish, busting the two bottom buttons in the process. He made quick work of his pants, then lassoed her by the waist. Seizing her mouth, he lifted her to his middle and straddled her to him. Her delta felt as hot and wet as her mouth tasted. And he couldn't wait to see for himself.

He carried her to the bed and laid her down, her breath catching in her throat at the sight of his burgeoning erection. Wholehearted superlatives escaped her lips as she extended her arms, inviting his throbbing body to hers. Suddenly Mike didn't know what to do; where to start. He was still trying to collect himself when Delaney all but bit the air and purred, "Mike, come to me."

"Not until you come first," he decided out loud. Kneeling, he gently pried her legs apart and pressed his mouth to her smooth triangle. He burrowed his face into her creamy pleats and began to lick. Long, lazy strokes at first, then short, quick ones. His fingers picked up where his tongue left off, leaving his mouth free to explore her even deeper. He sucked her center and she began to seep, her head shooting back like a piston as he devoured her. She arched on the bed, allowing him access to all her folds. Her fingers curled on the bed sheets as he explored every crease and crevice of her fleshy core. Her breaths came in short spurts, her utterances of appreciation became cries of pleasure, her pelvis began to rock above him as the arch of gratification built inside her. He felt her begin to quiver even before she tightened her knees around his head and screamed his name. Her flailing hands froze in his hair as she surrendered to the spasms.

Drenching him and quaking, she peaked, nearly taking him with him. Spent, Mike rested his head on her stomach, damp with sweat. Her pulse was quickening in her abdomen and her breaths were strangulated. She was still wallowing in the orgasm. And he was still reveling in giving it to her.

Her eyes fluttered open. "That was amazing." Her voice was blissfully exhausted. "I've never come that hard before."

He crawled up to her. "I almost came tasting you," he told her around a powerful, openmouthed kiss.

She returned the kiss, then eased him aside and started shimmying down the bed. "Now let me return the favor."

"Laney." He caught her arm. "I won't last long."

"We'll see about that." His cock was leaking readiness as she took hold of him. She gripped him at the base of his shaft and began to lick. Up and down her tongue meandered, finally pausing at the oozing tip. Taking the length of him in her mouth, she began to suck.

His groans filled the air as she consumed him. He felt his midsection jolt forward, his neck snap back, his eyes roll back in his head. It was beyond any arousal that he'd never known. And it was the only thing that could rival being inside her. He could feel the pressure intensifying, his meter pounding, the flow building. He was more than hard enough to make love to her. After a brief internal debate, he tapped her head. "Laney, now. I want to come inside you."

She slithered up to him with a contented smile and eyes dark with desire. He positioned her on her side next to him and entered her from behind. Their low growls merged into one hedonic moan as all of him met her soaking wet center. Pressing his palms against her breasts, Mike bent his knees and pushed against her. She circled his neck with her arms and they fell into a voluptuous, instinctual rhythm. Back and forth they swayed, her head tucked into the crook of his shoulder and the small of her back grinding against his stomach. He heard her baiting breaths against his cheek, her burning appeals in his ear. And just as she began to shatter, he drained himself into her.

CHAPTER FIFTEEN

SOMETIMES THINGS JUST WORK out. Who would have thought that picking up a secondhand newspaper would prove so prolific. Not to mention that it was open to the society column, a section of the paper Watson rarely perused. And the brunette staring back at him from the crinkled page of *The Chronicle* looked a helluva lot like Delaney Richards. Reaching into his pocket, he retrieved the headshot and juxtaposed the pictures. She had a glint in her chocolate brown eyes and her smile was wider, more heartfelt than in the photograph he had, but it was definitely her. He shifted his gaze to the man in the tux standing next to her. The caption cited him as Michael Savoy, III, son of Michael and Patricia Savoy, longtime supporters of The Entrepreneurs Charity Ball. The man appeared to be at least a decade older and was holding her close with his arm planted firmly around her waist.

Like a lover.

"Welcome to Lori's," a perky young woman interrupted his thoughts, pulling a small notebook out of her apron pocket. "Can I bring you something to drink while you decide on breakfast?"

"Coffee, please. And I'll have the special."

Nodding in acknowledgement, she made a notation on the pad and walked away.

He returned to the picture and the accompanying article. The gala had been held at the

Fairmont Hotel, confirming his preliminary information. Had she checked in, checked out and then in again? He reached for his phone and pulled up the hotel's web site.

"Thank you for calling the Fairmont Hotel, San Francisco. How may I direct your call?"

"Delaney Richards' room, please."

There was a moment of silence, then the singsong voice replied. "I'm sorry, sir. No one by that name is registered."

He glanced back at the newspaper. "How about Michael Savoy?"

"Uh...yes, one moment please. I'll connect you."

"Thank you." Suspicions confirmed, he disconnected before the second ring. He didn't remember the name Michael Savoy in any of the intelligence he'd gathered on Richards or the girl. He was punching the name into Safari when the waitress returned with the coffee. "Oh, did I miss The Entrepreneurs Charity Ball?" she remarked sarcastically, gesturing toward the paper. "I guess my invitation got lost in the mail again."

"Looks like a fancy party for rich folks with too much time on their hands."

She shrugged indifferently. "There are worse things to do with your time than raise money for the less fortunate. I think it's ten thousand dollars just to get in the door. And a donation on top of that."

"Must be nice. The highlight of my week was going to the Giants game."

"No kidding." She shifted her gaze over his head to the sounds of entry at the front of the restaurant. "Your food will be right up," she said, taking her leave.

Watson returned his attention to his phone. His search had brought up dozens of Michael Savoys in San Francisco. He scrolled down and clicked on a profile about a pioneering young businessman who began the first weekly garbage collection company in the city after the War. His son had sold it to a conglomerate for an unreported sum years later.

The waitress' voice over his shoulder interrupted his thoughts. "Here you go. Anything else I can get for you, sir?"

"Just a box," he told her, reaching into his back pocket for his wallet. "I'm going to have to take this to go."

Sometimes things just work out.

෮

"I trust your stay was enjoyable, Mr. Savoy."

"Very much so," Mike told the clerk with an inward smile.

"Charge the card on file?"

"Yeah."

Nodding in acknowledgement, the young woman returned to the keyboard and after a few seconds, slid a receipt into an envelope and handed it to him. "Thank you. We'll look forward to seeing you again."

"Indeed," Mike replied, shoving the envelope into his jacket pocket. When he turned around, Charlie was approaching him from the opposite side of the lobby.

"Mr. Savoy!"

Mike met him halfway. "Hello, Charlie."

"I'm glad I caught you. When I noticed your car was still here, I assumed you'd checked in after all." His gaze took in the near distance, then he inquired, "Is Ms. Richards with you?"

"She'll be down shortly."

Charlie leaned forward conspiratorially. "I saw that man again this morning. The one who was looking for her the other day."

Mike felt the hair on the back of his neck stand up. "Did he ask about her again?"

"Not that I know of. I only saw him in passing. He was leaving as I was coming on shift."

"Did you notice where he went?"

"He was on foot, heading south. I tried your cell."

Mike gave himself a mental kick for ignoring the unknown number earlier. "You're sure it was the same guy?"

"Positive," Charlie assured him, then sent a tight nod over Mike's shoulder. "Maybe Marisol saw him. She was in before me."

Charlie on his heels, Mike instantly retraced his steps.

"Can I help you with something further, Mr. Savoy?"

"I hope so. I understand you've been here all morning?"

"Since six o'clock."

The two men exchanged a look of camaraderie, then Charlie described the man he'd seen earlier.

"There was a gentleman fitting that description here this morning, but he wasn't asking for anyone. He dropped off that envelope for Mr. Savoy."

Mike cocked his head in confusion and narrowed his eyes. "What envelope?"

"The one I gave you with your receipt," she told him matter-of-factly, then clarified,

"Actually, he asked for an envelope, which I provided. Another guest needed assistance and by the time I helped them, he was gone. The envelope was sitting there with your name on it, so I put it aside for you."

Mike reached into his pocket and retrieved the envelope. When he tore open one end, a newspaper clipping fell out.

"Oh, look, it's you!" Marisol exclaimed, leaning over the desk. "What a good picture. I would have recognized you even without the tux."

But it wasn't the picture Mike was looking at. It was the sloppy handwriting next to it.

Beautiful picture, beautiful girl. To keep her that way, meet me at Pier 39 tonight at six o'clock. Come alone.

Mike was still staring at the photo, dumbfounded, when he heard Charlie say, "Marisol, call Security. We're gonna need to see the surveillance tape from this morning."

❧

"I can't do that, Mike. Even for you."

"Bullshit," Mike told Nick Camden an hour later outside the security office of the Fairmont. "There's always a way."

"There hasn't been a crime or even a credible threat. I can't allocate resources without something more."

"Fine. I'll provide the resources."

"Only off duty cops can take side jobs. And since it's a parade weekend in high season, everybody is on duty or on call."

"So what do you suggest I do? Sit around and wait for something to happen? *Then* call the police?"

"That's what the cop in me is saying. As your friend, however, I'm offering to go with you to meet this joker and see what he's after. More than likely he figures you for deep pockets, thinks he has something on you, wants to capitalize. We'll make quick work of it and grab a beer afterwards."

"No, this isn't about me," Mike corrected him. "There's more to it. Someone was here looking for Delaney before our picture was published in *The Chronicle*."

Nick started with a reluctant sigh. "How much do you know about this girl anyway?"

Mike heard the insinuation in the other man's voice. "I know all I need to know about her."

"And how much does she know about you? About your family, your holdings." He gave Mike a leery look.

"She only knows what I told her."

"Which was?"

"Very little. She's wouldn't care about any of that anyway."

"You sure? Did you run her?"

"What?"

"Did you check her out? C'mon, Mike, think about it. She waltzes into your life one day and ends up at the wedding of a mutual friend the next. Quite a coincidence. Next thing you know, she's visiting you in San Francisco, meeting your family, getting you all tied up in knots. Does she know you work purely out of choice? That your aging parents live off the interest of your family fortune and are saving the principle for generations to come? Not a bad hand to deal into to."

"Go to hell, Nick."

Nick's thin mouth tightened before he backed down a little. "Okay, maybe I deserved that. But hear me out. I came by the gambling analogy honestly." He reached into his breast pocket, retrieved a folded stack of papers and handed them to Mike. "I did a little checking before I headed over here. Delaney Richards' father has done hard time. Felony theft, bank fraud, illegal gambling. Served a dime at Folsom. Just got paroled."

Mike didn't spare the papers a glance. "She hasn't seen her father since she was two. She doesn't even remember him."

Nick nodded slowly, then got to the point. "Maybe not, but he remembers her. Apparently he's watched her grow up from afar. None too quietly either. One of my snitches knew Richards on the inside. Said he was proud as a peacock of his baby girl."

"So?"

"So, Colton Richards wasn't just a con artist and a thief. He had a gambling problem. He owes some serious people some big money. And some of the money he stole was never recovered. Supposedly he hid it somewhere in the mountains."

"What does that have to do with Delaney?"

"Whoever has Richards by the balls is gonna want their money. If he's smart enough to survive a decade in prison, he's too smart to lead them to the stash. They need a bargaining chip."

Mike felt a shiver trickle down his spine.

"And if Richards doesn't roll," Nick pushed on, "now they've got you for insurance. Or an unexpected bonus, depending on how you look at it."

"Sorry for the delay, gentlemen." A short man with a receding hairline and a potbelly interrupted their conversation. "I'm John Duggan, head of hotel security."

Mike introduced himself and returned the firm handshake. "Nice to meet you."

Then the older man extended his hand to Nick. "Good to see you again. Congrats on making lieutenant."

"Thanks. Had to give up the off duty gigs, though."

"Price of progress, I guess. Come on in," he invited with a wave of the hand.

The two men followed John into what appeared to be a renovated hotel suite. Three uniformed guards were sitting in front of a bank of TV monitors. "We've got constant surveillance of the perimeter of the property stored for seven days," he explained. "The common interior areas are on a twenty-four hour loop." He addressed one of the guards. "Bring up 0900 hours." The young man obliged as John kept talking. "Charlie reviewed the footage from this morning and identified this man as the one who inquired about Ms. Richards the other day."

Mike and Nick watched as a man fitting the description Charlie had provided approached the front desk and exchanged pleasantries with Marisol. The camera held for a few seconds, then began its rotation of the lobby. By the time it came back full circle the man was gone.

"He couldn't have been here more than five minutes," John informed them. "That's how long it the camera takes to sweep the lobby."

"Can you go back and freeze the frame?" Nick asked the guard.

"Sure."

Nick leaned forward and narrowed his eyes. "I don't recognize him. Must be from out of town. Send it to my phone. I'll see if they can get a facial recognition hit downtown."

"Will do," the guard replied as Nick relayed the number.

Then Nick straightened up and addressed John. "Thanks for your time."

"No problem."

"That's it?" Mike objected, appalled. "That's all we have to go on? That's all we're going to do?"

Nick and John exchanged a knowing look. Then the latter said, "I'm sorry I couldn't help more. We'll keep an eye out for him. But since Ms. Richards is no longer staying here, chances are he won't be back."

John escorted them to the door and showed them out. When they were out in the hallway again, Mike asked Nick, "Now what?"

"Now I see if he's in the system. If that's possible from the distorted black and white image we have to go on."

"Fine. I'll go with you."

Nick summoned the elevator. "No, you'll go home and wait to hear from me. This is on the Q.T., remember?"

Mike opened his mouth to argue, then thought better of it. Delaney was safer with him anyway. "Okay," he conceded as the elevator arrived. For now, he silently added.

❧

"No, ma'am." The woman waved away the bills. "The tip has already been taken care of."

"Thank you," Delaney said, seeing her to the door. As if this wasn't already the happiest morning of her life, Mike had called and surprised her with a massage in the room.

After the masseuse left, Delaney loosened the spa robe and fell onto the king-size bed, wishing Mike was there with her. She'd woken up first this morning, surrounded by a sea of pillows and rumpled sheets. And the sweet scent of love making. He'd been laying on his side with a lazy arm draped over her. If not for his steady breathing in her ear, she'd sworn she was dreaming. She tried not to wonder how many women had woken up in Mike's arms. Certainly enough for him to know what he was doing in bed. But he'd looked at her so profoundly when he climaxed that she'd felt like the only one. She wanted him to make love to her like that every night for the rest of their lives. And incredibly, he wanted that too. He'd all but proposed last night. She let the joy wash over her. She'd taken the chance, let herself love again. Now she had a lifetime of love to look forward to.

"Laney?" called Mike from the living room.

"In here."

"Sorry that took so long." He plopped down next to her. "Charlie's in love with my car. I figured this was as good a time as any to take him for a spin since you weren't ready yet. But one thing led to another and the next thing I knew, we were at Fort Mason."

"No problem. The massage was wonderful. And you probably gave Charlie the thrill of his life."

He laid a kiss on her lips. "Yeah. I know the feeling."

She returned the smile, but felt it fade when she noticed the reservation in his eyes. "Is everything okay?"

"Yeah, why?"

"You look worried all the sudden."

"Just tired." Then he slid his hand into the robe and turning his body to hers, hooked her waist. He held her against him for a long moment, then with a kiss on the forehead, said,

"C'mon, let's go home."

Delaney relished him, in them, in the feeling of going home for the first time in so long. But that portentous feeling was creeping into the pit of her stomach again. Scolding herself for perpetually waiting for the other shoe to drop, she pushed it down and got up to get dressed.

CHAPTER SIXTEEN

"I'M SORRY ABOUT THIS," Mike told Delaney later that afternoon. "It shouldn't take too long."

"No problem. Does this happen every time there's a potential terrorism threat?" she inquired. "Even overseas?"

"No, but whenever we implement heightened security procedures, we're briefed as our schedule allows. And since I'm off, my number came up. It's kinda like random drug testing." Mike picked up his wallet and keys from the kitchen counter. "While I'm gone, decide where you want to have dinner. It'll be a little later by the time I get back, so we'll miss the Saturday night rush."

"In that case, I'll do some shopping. I want to pick something up for—"

"No!" Mike cut her off. "We can do that later. Together."

"But there's no sense in spending our last night souvenir shopping when I could take care of it now."

He grabbed her by the forearms. "Just stay here." His tone was as stern as his eyes were fierce. Delaney's stomach began that familiar churn. "Mike, you're scaring me. What's going on?"

"There's nothing going on." The forced smile stalled at the corners of his mouth. "And it's not our last night."

"You know what I mean."

"Just stay here until I get back." He gathered her to him and held her longer than he needed to. "Promise me."

"Okay," she said, as the angst brewing in her stomach moved to her throat.

"I love you, Laney."

"I love you, too."

She watched his retreating back and locked the door behind him, then started to pace around the living room. Something was wrong. Delaney could feel it in her bones. Mike had been distracted and restless ever since they left the hotel. And now something had suddenly come up at work. She searched the street below, expecting to see Mike's car pull out. Instead she saw him exit the building on foot. She trailed him with her eyes until he disappeared around the corner. Apparently he'd changed his mind about driving to the airport. Had he also changed his mind about her? Like Ryan and her father? No, even worse. Because a liar is worse than a coward.

She plopped down on the couch with helpless sigh. There'd been a shift in him, subtle as it was. What had suddenly changed? Was it her performance in bed last night? The fact that tomorrow she'd be two thousand miles away? Or had the infatuation simply passed?

No, she wouldn't let herself believe that.

Their connection had been instant, visceral, mutual. She knew she truly loved him, believed that he truly loved her. So why was he acting so out of character? She dabbed at the hot tears stinging her eyes. One thing was for sure, she wasn't going to find out sitting around here.

Grabbing her purse, she headed out the door.

The late afternoon sky was overcast and the air chilly, despite the sun's repeated attempts to break through. Taking in the street, Delaney swore under her breath. This was as far as her plan went, so she decided to walk in the direction Mike had taken. Intuition told her all of this had something to do with the man asking about her at the Fairmont. Although that certainly hadn't affected Mike's demeanor last night. She hadn't thought anything of it at the time, but it was odd that he had suddenly sent up a massage this morning. It was as if he was handling her, keeping her busy. Or, she was starting to believe, protecting her.

But from what?

He'd been conveniently and unexpectedly called into work. And had taken off down the street on foot like a bat out of hell. Right after he'd said that he loved her, more intensely than warranted for a few hours apart. After carefully reminding her that this wasn't their last night together. With soulful eyes that begged her to wait for him at home. So what was she doing? Isn't blind trust the true test of love? To put complete and total faith in someone? To follow your heart instead of your head? Who was the liar now? She'd promised to stay put. But the past had jaded her. She wasn't the one who had given up; she'd been given up on. And she wasn't going to be a hypocrite and do the same. She loved Mike more than she thought possible. And that was worth fighting for. The risk of losing her heart was worth the reward of keeping his.

Sorely disappointed in herself for doubting him, for doubting them, Delaney turned on her heel and began retracing her steps. Resolve amplifying with each footstep, she kicked it into double-time. Lost in thought, she had to stop abruptly at a crosswalk for a changing signal. So much so that someone nearly bumped into her from behind. "Sorry," she threw over her shoulder, laser-focused on getting back to Mike's. She would call him and they would straighten this whole thing out.

The signal changed and she began walking across the street. A man was quickly approaching on her left side, she noticed out of the corner of her eye. It was likely the same person who'd almost bumped into her. He smelled of the sea and yesterday's cologne and was walking directly behind her, even though his legs could easy outstride her. Her eyes scanned the street, oddly free of pedestrians, as a cable car noisily approached. She picked up her pace as that ominous feeling returned, this time sending a shiver up her spine. Panic tugged at her stomach and her heart beat in her ears as the footsteps behind her quickened and the man suddenly appeared beside her. The cable car whizzed by and she felt its breeze cross her face. Then a large hand gripped her arm. And everything went black.

❧

"I thought I told you to stay home." Nick reminded Mike firmly.

"What makes you think I didn't?" Mike decided to head west and take the longer, less conspicuous route. This bastard had the advantage of knowing what he looked like.

"Hunch," he replied. "You took my direction way too easily. The more I thought about it, the more I knew you wouldn't wait around for a call. Plus I put eyes on you."

"I thought you were tight on resources."

"Something opened up."

"Then assign him to the case. I have an appointment to keep."

"Not anymore you don't."

Mike sucked in a sharp breath. "Did you find him?"

"Yeah, we found him. But he's not taking any meetings. Head toward the Marina. I'll be waiting."

Mike pivoted on his heel and headed north. And not fifteen minutes later found himself staring at a dead man.

"Watson Brewer, age 52. Never been married, never enlisted in the Service, never applied for a loan. Expired Nevada driver's license; LVPD are going over to the last known address now," Nick informed Mike. They stood along the Embarcadero as waves of gray cotton layered the waterfront and the smell of rotten fish hovered in the air. After pausing for a breath he resumed reading from his phone screen. "Was in and out of juvie, then seemed to be on the straight and narrow for a while. An occasional misdemeanor, a little time here and there. Fell off the grid all together about ten years ago." He looked up at Mike. "Recognize him?"

Mike pushed away the nausea. He'd never seen a dead body before. "Looks like the guy from the surveillance tape." And somewhere else Mike couldn't quite put his finger on.

"Forensics will confirm that. But I'm more concerned about what brought Mr. Brewer to our fair city. He's never held a job outside of Clark County, Nevada, never been out of the country or in the hospital. Used a fresh credit card to buy an airline ticket from McCarran to SFO last week. We're checking with some of the low-end motels in the area to see where he was staying."

"And?" Mike asked the bothersome hesitation in Nick's voice.

"And." Nick strung out the word. "Brewer's a known associate of Frank Sansome."

Mike shot Nick a baffled look and threw up his hands. "Should that mean something to me?"

"Only if you follow the money laundering trade in Vegas." Nick returned his phone to his breast pocket and started walking. "It means Brewer's stock just went up in my book."

"I'm listening," said Mike, falling into step beside him.

"Frank Sansome is an old school, eye for an eye type of crook. Plays for keeps, pretends to forgive, but never forgets. Colton Richards ran with his gang, pulled jobs for him. If he skimmed off the top, there's gonna be hell to pay. To save face if nothing else. Sansome will get his money. One way or the other."

Mike's head was spinning. "What does that have to do with Delaney?"

"Richards left Folsom six days ago. Chances are he'll lay low for a while, check in with his P.O. as scheduled, bag groceries, etc. If there's a hidden stash, he won't go for it right away.

Sansome is wise to that. Takes one to know one."

"So where does Brewer fit in?"

"Sansome hires Brewer to do some reconnaissance, speed things along. Find the girl, follow the girl, remind Richards of what he's got to lose."

"He hasn't seen Delaney in over twenty-five years. Why does he care?"

Nick shot Mike a oblique grin. "That's right, you don't have kids. Because she's all he's got. Maybe he wants a stab at making amends."

Or maybe the bastard just wants to get the money and disappear, Mike thought as his stomach fell one more notch.

"Then why kill Brewer?"

"I'm still a little foggy on that. It seems a little rash for Sansome. He's usually more prudent. But guys like Brewer sell to the highest bidder, including themselves. He found out about you, saw an opportunity to double his money. Or cut Sansome out all together. Maybe Sansome got wise to that, confronted him and it escalated."

Mike looked out over the water unseeingly, as a symphony of sea lions barked in the distance. "How do we find this Sansome?"

"He'll find you. That's what worries me. Where's Delaney now?"

"At my place. I told her I had an emergency meeting at the airport. Homeland Security stuff." Stuffing his hands in his pockets, he kicked the ground. "I hated lying to her, but it was all I could come up with."

"Did she buy it?"

"Yeah, but she was suspicious when I told her to stay put. She wanted to go shopping."

Nick's ruddy face crinkled into a dubious frown. "You've known this girl what, a week?"

Mike could feel the indignation brewing again. "We've been over this, Nick. What are you getting at?"

"You can't ignore the possibility she's in on it."

Mike didn't wait for his brain to catch up with his fist, but he watched it skim the corner of Nick's left eye. His aim was better the second time, but Nick thwarted it, then pinned Mike's arms behind his back.

"What the hell's wrong with you?" Nick asked through gritted teeth. "This place is crawling with cops. You're gonna get yourself shot."

"How many times do I have to tell you? Delaney has nothing to do with this," Mike spat over his shoulder.

"Try something like that again and I'll book you for assault," Nick warned, releasing him with a shove. "Nice right hook, though."

Mike shook it off. "So, are you gonna help me or not?" He sounded as achingly desperate as he felt inside.

"I have no choice but to help you now," Nick told him. "This is a homicide. My specialty."

CHAPTER SEVENTEEN

DELANEY'S HEAD WAS THROBBING, pounding at the temples and being squeezed into a vise at the crown. She blinked hard a few times and her eyes adjusted slowly, as if coming out of a long, dark tunnel. She was lying on a hard bed in a dimly lit room, with only a slice of light coming from under a door. Sitting up, she lifted her gaze to the sound of pages turning. She saw a woman sitting in the corner, thumbing through a magazine.

Panic began to rise inside her and tears welled in her eyes as it all came rushing back. Talking herself off the ledge, the certainty she'd felt about going back to Mike's apartment to wait for him, the man behind, then beside her. And the hot prick in her arm. She was still dressed in the jeans and sweater set she'd changed into earlier and she patted the front pockets for her phone, inadvertently alerting the woman. Automatically defensive, Delaney pulled the cardigan tighter around her. Swallowing the fear that threatened to strangle her and clenching her fists, she tried to steel herself as the woman approached the bed.

"You okay? Your head hurt?"

She was more of a girl than a woman, Delaney realized, easing a bit. She was slight of build, with delicate features and short, pixie-like hair. And the darkest black eyes Delaney had seen. All she could do was nod, following the woman's movements with aching eyes as she walked over and opened the cracked door all the way. Harsh, white light flooded the tiny room. She was in a hotel, Delaney realized. And it sure as hell wasn't the Fairmont. The room was dingy and sparsely furnished with a dilapidated dresser, the bed she was laying on and a drop leaf table with two spindle-legged chairs. She watched the woman enter the bathroom and fill a glass with water, then approach her again.

"Here," she said, handing Delaney the glass and two capsules. "Take this."

Delaney's initial reaction was no way in hell, but her head was hurting so much she could barely see straight. And that was not conducive to getting out of here. She looked down at the pills, and recognizing their brownish color, decided to go with the lesser of the two evils. She swallowed them gingerly, never taking her eyes off her companion.

As if reading Delaney's mind, the woman spoke in broken English. "It's okay. No one hurt you here."

"Where am I?" Delaney asked, scanning the room. "Who are you?"

"You in Chinatown. I'm Ali. I sit with you until Mister comes back. Make sure you're okay."

"Mister? Mister who?"

Ali's shoulders lifted and fell in uncertainty. "Just Mister. We stay here until he comes back with the money."

Delaney couldn't fathom what she was talking about. "Money? What money?"

"The money your father stole from him."

"My *father*?" Delaney marveled.

"Yeah," she explained matter-of-factly. "He wouldn't give it back, so Mister had to do something to make him. That's why he take you. To make him listen."

Delaney rubbed her temples and let out a shallow breath. She was even more confused than before. "You're holding me for ransom? From my father?"

"Yes, because he needs incentive," Ali finished proudly, dragging out the word.

Delaney could only shake her head in utter disbelief. "You must have me confused with someone else."

"No." She pointed to a photograph on the table. "This is you, right?"

Delaney stared at it in bewilderment, then held it in her hand for a closer look. It was the headshot from *Crain's*, announcing she's been appointed interim vice-president. She wondered if this was the picture Charlie had seen. "Yes, but I haven't seen my father in twenty-five years." She pushed the photograph away.

Ali's angelic face became a dark frown. "You haven't?"

"No."

"Then how will Mister get the money?"

He won't. She had to get out of here before this man came back. She pushed down the terror and began in a disturbingly reasonable voice. "I don't know. Maybe I could help him."

Ali gave her a curious look. "How?"

"I have some money of my own." Delaney straightened up conspiratorially. "We could go get it."

Ali's eyes narrowed in suspicion. "No. Mister said we can't leave. The door is locked from the outside anyway."

Delaney shifted her gaze to the deadbolts on the door, then to the narrow window. "Maybe the window, then. Let's try," she suggested gamely, rising.

"No!" Ali exclaimed.

Jumping her ran briefly through Delaney's mind, but she instantly thought better of it. She could barely think, had no idea where she was or how to get help. If she could earn Ali's trust, maybe she would become an inadvertent ally. "Okay, okay." She held her hands out in the air in front of her. "It was just an idea. You know, to solve our little problem."

"Our problem?" she asked, cocking her head to the side.

Delaney could feel the Advil kicking in, attacking the headache and further emboldening her. "Yeah. If Mister comes back without the money, he won't be able to pay you. But I could pay you, if we went to get to my money."

Delaney looked on as Ali processed the words, then weighed them. After a long moment, she concluded, "But Mister will be mad."

"Maybe. But won't whomever you're giving the money to be mad too?" Delaney went with her gut. "If you go home without it?"

That seemed to resonate with her. "Yeah. We need money for rent and food," Ali reminded herself out loud. She glanced at the window. "But the window has bars."

Delaney tried to hide her disappointment. "Let me look." This time Ali didn't stop her when she stood. Hands shaking, she walked over to the window and pulled back the threadbare curtains. The bars were broken in places and bowed in others. She might be able to squeeze through and jump to the fire escape. She took in the stingy view; they were definitely in Chinatown. The street was lit by paper lanterns strung across the dark alleyway below. Hope wrangled with the fear, fueling her moxie. She had no other choice. Because, as usual, Delaney was on her own.

☙

"Laney, I'm back. Did you decide on dinner?" Mike called out, eyes sweeping the apartment. The low, gray ceiling of the sky cast an eerie, hollow hue on the living room, paralleling the feeling tethered to his gut for the last few hours. "Turned out to be a false alarm. I didn't even make it past Daly City."

"Laney?" Mike repeated, stomach dropping. "Laney?" Running through the house, he came up empty. "Laney!" He was going for his phone when it started ringing. "Yeah!"

"You're welcome," Nick said by way of greeting.

Mike couldn't imagine what for. He blew out a frustrated breath. "For what?"

"There'll be a plainclothes man in front of your building within thirty minutes. He'll check in with you periodically."

"That's not going to work, Nick."

"That's the best I can do. A full security detail is out of the question."

"It's not going to work because I'm not going to be there." Mike flew out of the apartment, heading for the elevator. "I'm leaving to find Delaney."

There was a momentary lull, during which Mike pictured Nick shooting up from behind his desk. "She's not at your place?"

Where was the goddamn elevator? "No!" He screamed into the phone, running toward the stairs.

"I don't like the sound of that." His voice was grave now. "Not at all." Nick took a purposeful breath, then released it hard through his nose.

"Mike, we can't ignore the possibility that she's in on—"

"Hold on! That's her!" Mike interrupted. Heart leaping out of his chest, he switched calls. "Laney!"

"Try again, Mr. Savoy."

The voice was rough, weathered by life and laced with arrogance. And when Mike didn't say anything, it kept going. "Mr. Savoy? Are you there?"

"Who the hell is this?"

"It doesn't matter who I am," the man said. "Only what I have. And I have something of yours."

Mike instantly felt sick, but willed his voice level. "Really? I'm not missing anything."

"I find that hard to believe. Ms. Richards is quite lovely. And you appear to be quite smitten with her."

"Hardly." Mike clenched his jaw and pressed his eyes closed. "We've only just met."

The caller made a tsking sound. "Imagine how disappointed she'll be when I tell her she means so little to you."

Mike was starting to catch on. "How much should she mean?"

"Oh, a million dollars or so."

"A *million* dollars?"

"Pocket change for you, Mr. Savoy. That will satisfy her debt and give me a little something for my trouble."

"What debt could she possibly owe you?"

"Sins of the father and all that," he replied dismissively. "Get the money together. I'll be in touch."

"Wait!" Mike pleaded more than he liked. "You know my name, but I don't know yours."

"That's not by accident. And not subject to change." After an interminable silence, he added, "Of course, this is just between the two of us. No cops." There was a click, followed by dead air, then the steady beep of disconnection.

Mike switched back to Nick. "I just got a ransom call."

"Don't do anything. I'll be right there."

But Mike was already reversing course, taking the steps two at a time. He stormed back into his apartment and headed for the bedroom. "Suit yourself."

"Don't do this." Nick was still talking, becoming increasingly breathless. "I'm begging you."

"I don't have a choice."

"Sure you do. He needs you more than you need him."

"No, I need *her*. She's all that matters to me."

"Mike, blackmail never ends well if you take away the currency. As long as she's an asset, she's safe. And as long as you have the money, she's an asset. The moment that changes, we have a problem."

"We already have a problem!" Mike yelled into the phone, throwing clothes from the back rack of the bedroom closet on the floor. "A big fucking problem! And I'm going to solve it. My way."

"The hell you are! Your way could get you and her killed. And maybe even me, backing up your sorry ass." There was a banging on the apartment door. "Open your goddam door. I'm here."

Later it would occur to Mike that Nick was the plainclothes man that had suddenly been assigned to the case. Throwing the phone on the bed, he sprinted to the door. He opened it and without sparing Nick a glance, returned to the bedroom and the matter at hand.

Nick was on his heels. He stood beside him now, clothes strewn on the closet floor at their feet. "Are you telling me that you have a million dollars in cash behind this wall?"

"Of course not!" Mike spun the dial for the third time.

"Then what the hell are you doing?"

"I have some cash, plus stocks, annuities, commercial paper that can be turned into cash."

"On a Saturday night?"

"No, but I could offer them up as collateral, liquidate them on Monday." Sooner if he involved his father. He usually kept cash around.

"You think Sansome is going to go for that? And leave a paper trail?"

Mike let out a defeated breath and hung his head. Nick was right and he knew it. "What else can I do?"

"You can listen to reason, let us do our job. We know Brewer was on foot. He had to be staying somewhere nearby. Where paying cash wouldn't raise any eyebrows."

"Like half of San Francisco."

Nick grunted away the snarky half-exaggeration. "If Brewer was dumb enough to get himself killed, he might have been dumb enough to register in his own name. Sansome doesn't know we know who Brewer is, let alone know that he's dead. He may let his guard down and assume his identity. If we can get a step ahead of him, we can beat him at his own game."

"But we're the ones playing catch-up."

"I know it seems that way. But—"

"It is that way!" Mike cut him off. "How can you be sure we're dealing with this Sansome to begin with?"

"I can't," Nick conceded. "Not yet anyway. We need to buy some time."

"How the hell do we do that?"

"Ask for proof."

"Of what?"

"That Sansome, or anyone else, really has her."

"The ransom call came from her phone!"

"Exactly. For all you know she's playing you for a fool. There's no sign of forced entry here."

Mike clenched his fists and ground his teeth. "She's not in on it, Nick. Get that through your fucking head."

"I'm starting to believe that. I've known you a long time, have never seen you like this." Nick gave him a long, hard stare. Then he said, "I have another idea, but you aren't gonna like it."

As if Mike liked any of it. "What?"

"Convince Sansome she doesn't mean anything to you."

"What about her being an asset?"

"It's a risk, but it might help us gain the upper hand quickly." Nick slanted his head to one side in conjecture and continued, "You pretend to cooperate, but show up empty-handed. We trap him and he gives her up."

Mike noted the borrowed conviction in his friend's voice. "Or?"

"We go by the book, double down. You don't show at all, but we do. We tail him, he leads us to her. Hopefully we can secure her while he resorts to the original plan, finding Richards and the stash. But he'll no doubt tell her you refused to pay the ransom if we don't get to her first. And I'll warn you he's—" The trill of Nick's phone filled the room. "Camden. Yeah....Good work. Bring Findley in on it. He's got connections there."

Momentarily encouraged, Mike looked on as the other man listened, then asked, "Are you sure? Was he in jewelry?" Nick's eyes darted back and forth furiously. "Let me know the second you get an ID." Ending the call, he took an exasperated hand to his forehead.

"Now what?"

"Colton Richards didn't check in with his P.O. this morning."

"Shocker. So much for your make amends theory," Mike snickered.

"Maybe not. A John Doe was found dead in a bus station in Vegas. The victim of an apparent heart attack."

"So?"

"So Mr. Doe had nearly a quarter million dollars in cash on him."

"Can't be the first time that's happened in Vegas."

"He fits Colton Richards' description. We'll have confirmation within an hour."

Mike wasn't sure what difference that made, but he sensed it wasn't good. "Which means…"

"There's no time for half-measures now. No buying time. Once Sansome finds out that Richards is dead, the ransom is his only option. And he's not known for his patience."

"So I'm going in empty-handed," Mike declared, as the trepidation surging through him snuck into his voice. "It's showtime."

CHAPTER EIGHTEEN

THE WINDOW WOULDN'T BUDGE, as if it had been painted shut. Delaney blew away the disappointment and tried again. She was wondering if things could get any worse when the sound of quickly approaching footfalls filled the air. And for what seemed like the hundredth time today, her heart lodged in her throat.

"Get away from the window!" Ali ordered in a whisper as the footsteps halted.

Delaney obeyed, returning to the bed in the corner. She looked on in horror as the locks clicked one by one and then released. She heard a woman's voice speaking briskly in Mandarin. Delaney watched as Ali, eyes on her toes, nodded in reverent understanding. After a few seconds, the door opened all the way and she let the woman in. She looked like an older version of Ali, with gray steaks in her coal-black hair and thin-skinned hands that reflected a lifetime of work. And behind her, taking up the entire door frame, was was the biggest, burliest man Delaney had ever seen. There was a split second of hope when Delaney let herself believe that Mike had somehow sent him. Then a second man burst in behind him with a gun in his hand and that hope reverted to terror. She tried to hide her fear and forced herself to take bated breaths as the first man approached her. He was hatchet-faced but his deep-set eyes were kind. After giving her a cursory once-over, he bent down and said, "Ms. Richards?"

"Yes." she answered tentatively, watching out of the corner of his eye as the second man surveyed the room, weapon drawn.

"I'm Detective Findley, SFPD. He flashed a badge hooked to his waistband. Are you okay?"

Delaney relaxed a little. "Yeah, I guess so."

"Clear!" the other man shouted, then joined them.

"This is Detective Jared," Findley introduced his counterpart, gesturing behind him with a spiked thumb.

Detective Jared tipped his head and replaced his gun at the same time. "Ma'am."

"Let the lieutenant know we've got her," Findley directed over his shoulder.

The other detective nodded, then spoke into the walkie-talkie attached to his collar.

"You're safe now," Findley addressed Delaney again. "We're going to get you out of here."

Delaney took his extended hand and stood. "Thank you," she said through a shaky sigh of relief. "How did you find me?"

"You can thank the lieutenant for that, Ma'am."

Every answer seemed to lead to another question. "The lieutenant?"

"Lieutenant Camden. He had a hunch. Sounds like it came down pretty fast. I was on another case when I caught this one, so I don't have the details. He'll fill in the blanks down at the station."

Delaney could only nod, having no other viable course of action. She could feel the adrenaline leaving her body and her head start to throb again.

"Do you need a doctor?"

"I don't know. I have a terrible headache."

"We'll get you checked out. Anything else?"

"Yes. Detective, can you take me home?"

❧

"Right on time, Mr. Savoy. I like that. "

"Not much traffic this time of night."

"No, I don't imagine so."

"Come out and see for yourself."

"Nice try," the caller responded through a sinister laugh. "Do you have the money?"

"Did you really think I could raise a million dollars in a few hours? On the weekend, no less."

"From what I was told, yes."

"Who told you that?" Mike spun around and scanned the boardwalk. There were a few people milling around the Wharf, none of whom were talking on the phone.

"An old friend."

"Who?"

"No one you know."

"I must know them, seeing how they know so much about me." Mike strung him along, trying to stretch out the call.

"That's neither here nor there. He is no longer relevant. Don't move a muscle."

There was dead air for a few seconds before Mike heard a splash in the near distance. Then a restricted number appeared on his phone. He switched over. "Yeah."

"Can't be too careful these days. With all the new technology and all. Now where were we? Oh yes, the money. I don't see a bag in your hand. Do you have it on your person? That could get messy."

Mike began with mocked indifference. "Actually, I'm having second thoughts about the whole thing. It seems like a high price to pay for a long weekend."

"I see." There was a weighted pause, then he continued evenly, "Well, then our business here is done."

"Wait!" Mike panicked and went totally off script. "Maybe if I could see her again I'd feel differently."

"Not without the money."

Mike couldn't wait to get his hands on this guy. He ground his teeth and willed himself to follow the plan. The John Doe in Las Vegas had been positively identified as Colton Richards. He was Delaney's only chance now. "That's going to take a little more time. Is she with you now?"

"The terms of the arrangement aren't open for discussion, Mr. Savoy. When I get my million, you'll get your girl."

Mike's attention was diverted to a text from Nick. *"Keep him going. We have her."*

Mike lifted his eyes to the sky in silent gratitude, then returned to the conversation more cavalierly. "On second thought, don't bother. Half the reason I came down here was because I felt sorry for her. You know, to see if there was something I could do to help her out. I have no feelings for her beyond the bedroom. And even that wasn't that memorable. Certainly not worth a—"

He stopped short when saw her. She was standing in the shadows wrapped in a blanket, gape-mouthed and wide-eyed. And hanging on his every word. But as impossible as the words had been to say, seeing the betrayal register on her shocked, despair-filled face was even more agonizing. This wasn't the one-dimensional pain he'd seen in her eyes before; this anguish penetrated her very soul. At that moment Mike realized how much she must love him, trust him. Enough to have dangled herself on that precipice for him and let herself fall. She was plummeting at his hand and he couldn't catch her. Not if he wanted to spend the rest of his life with her. Hoping she'd listen with her heart instead of her head, he went for broke, "million dollars."

"Again, I find that hard to believe. But I'll have to take your word for it. This is your last chance.

You have ten-seconds to reconsider. Nine, eight, seven, six,..."

The countdown was interrupted by the sounds of running footfalls and indistinct commands. Then Mike heard a loud thump and a disembodied voice shout, "Clear!" The night air exploded with blaring sirens and flashing lights. But Mike hardly noticed. All he cared about was Delaney. But the time he got over to where she'd been standing, she was gone.

◆

It had started out as the best day of her life, full of love and promise. And at long last, trust. And had ended as the worst. On cold, damp Fisherman's Wharf in the middle of the night. If she hadn't heard the words with her own ears, she wouldn't have believed them. She would have let a part of her go on believing that she was an unlikely pawn in some bizarre chess game. That the man looking for her at the hotel and the man who kidnapped her were no match for *her* man. She'd half-expected to find Mike standing on the street in Chinatown like he'd stood on Jackson the night she'd arrived from Tahoe. Or waiting in the police car like he'd waited for her to come back from dinner with Tom. Or pacing on the waterfront like he'd paced at the Fairmont when she was in the ladies room with his sisters.

But he wasn't.

"Laney!" Mike's repeated cries twisted the knife in her back straight through to her heart, effectively paralyzing her. She stood, statue-like, staring at the black ripples lapping at the boats as they creaked against the dock. She didn't turn toward the sound of his voice nor did she acknowledge it. "Laney!" He skidded to a stop behind her. She could hear his breathing level off and his heart beating outside of his chest as he whipped her around to face him. His eyes were feverish and wet. They searched hers frantically, while his hands ran up and down her arms, as if checking for injuries. "My God, Laney. Are you okay?" He took her in his arms and held on to her for dear life. She fell into him, suddenly drained and boneless. And so completely sure.

She felt him exhale and take a series of short breaths, as if catching up. They stood there, wrapped in each other and collectively weeping until Mike muttered, "I thought I lost you."

She inched back a little to meet his eyes. "I thought I lost *you*."

"That's impossible." He tipped her chin and brushed her lips with his. "Because I can't seem to function without you."

"Mike, I'm so confused."

"I'm not. None of it matters anyway. All that matters is that you're okay. I'll have plenty of time to explain it all to you. Because I'm never letting you out of my sight again."

"But the things you said..."

"Insurance," he interjected. "So we're not looking over our shoulder for the rest of our life. I had to keep him going until they had a visual." He cocked his head to the side and looked her dead in the eye. "Laney, how could you have thought otherwise?"

How could she have? "Because I'm an idiot. I'm sorry."

"Don't apologize. Just do me a favor."

She threw his arms around his neck. "What?" she asked as the tears, happy this time, built again.

His eyes danced waggishly. "The next time I tell you to stay home, listen.

CHAPTER NINETEEN

LESS THAN ONE WEEK later, Mike stood on the steps of Delaney's brownstone and scanned the street. They'd said six o'clock and it was quarter after. Even with Frank Sansome in jail and the missing money recovered, Laney being even a minute late sent his mind racing. He hit redial and assessed the fading light. The sky was about to open up. Her car was in the same spot as this morning, so maybe she'd taken the train to work after all. She was running late and her phone was dead, he reasoned inadequately and headed north toward the "L" stop. Shards of hail blanketed the sidewalk, crushing under his feet like glass. He would never get used to Midwestern thunderstorms. They come out of nowhere, wreak havoc and suddenly stop. A tremendous bolt of lightning painted the sky an uncanny eggplant color and the crackling of thunder over his shoulder was so impressive that he stopped and turned around. Just as Laney came skittering around the corner, head down and arms swaddled around her. It took him less than thirty seconds to change direction and be within arm's length of her. "Laney!"

Her head whipped up and she fell into his ams as the rain began to fall in sheets.

"Baby, are you okay?"

"I am now." Her voice was muffled, buried in his shoulder.

"Where were you?" Mike asked, leading her under the awning of a storefront.

"With Ryan."

Mike swore his heart stopped beating. "Your old boyfriend?"

"Fiancé," Delaney corrected him.

Hadn't they had enough of the past haunting them? "What did *he* want?"

"He didn't want anything. I asked him to meet me. I wanted to thank him."

"Thank him? For what? Putting you through hell?" Mike gathered her closer to shield her from the curtain of rain beating down around them.

"Yes, because if he hadn't changed his mind, we would have gone to Lindsay's wedding as man and wife. And there I would have met my soul mate, the love of my life, and realized I'd made the biggest mistake of my life. What would I have done then?"

She was drenched from head to toe, her hair was plastered against her head and streaks of makeup were running down her cheeks. And to Mike she'd never looked more beautiful. He felt his heart swell in his chest. "I don't know. I don't date married women. Unless they're married to me, of course. And until that night, I'd never met anyone I wanted to marry." He hadn't planned to ask her like this, on the street, in the rain, without the ring, but it just came out. "Will you marry me, Laney?"

Her eyes slanted up at the corners and began to shine. "Didn't I already say yes?"

"Not officially. We still have some logistical things to work out. Like where we're going to live. I know your job is very important to you. I can fly out of Chicago instead of San Francisco. When will you hear if you got the promotion?"

Her lips curved into a satisfied smile. "I already heard. The job is a dream. Complete autonomy, great bonus structure. Lots of freedom to implement my vision of where the company can go in the next five years."

"That's great!" Mike exclaimed, trying to sound enthusiastic. This would definitely be a challenge, but they would make it work somehow.

"Senior management didn't even interview anyone else," she went on loftily. "They had my offer letter and compensation package ready to be signed this morning."

The rain suddenly subsided and they began walking again. "Wow. That's awesome. I'm so proud of you."

"Thanks. You can imagine their surprise when I turned it down," she said offhandedly.

Jaw dropping, Mike stopped short. "You turned it down?"

"Uh-huh." She squeezed his hand. "Right before I quit."

"You quit?" he astonished.

"Yes, of course. How can I possibly do either one of those jobs from San Francisco?"

"Laney." He drew her to him, overcome by her willingness to sacrifice for them. "You don't have to do that. You've worked so hard to get where you are. You don't have to give it up. We'll figure it out."

"I'm not giving up, I'm getting. I don't want to commute across the country and only see you every other weekend, even temporarily. I don't want to work sixty hours a week and travel to trade shows every quarter."

"I don't want you to do that either, but it doesn't have to be all or nothing. We can live here and you can amend your hours. Come with me when I have layovers."

Delaney shook his words away. "You have your life, your job, your family in San Francisco. I used my job to escape my life because I was afraid to live it. I'm not afraid anymore. Because of you, I want to live my life, not run from it."

"Laney—"

"Besides," she plowed over him, "all I really have here is my mom and she's gone half the time, traveling for work or with girlfriends." She bit her lip, suddenly troubled. "But I won't have a job. Not for awhile, at least."

"Don't worry about that. I have plenty of money for us." Mike paused for effect. "And for whomever else may come along. That's another thing we haven't discussed. How many of us there are going to be."

He watched as she mentally debated, then reached a half-hearted conclusion. "I'd like to have a baby or two, but I understand if you don't. The most important thing is that we're together."

"So, let me get this straight," Mike said through a grin. "You not only turned down a huge promotion, but quit your job, are willing to move across the country and forego having kids for me?"

"I love you," she stated flatly. "I want a life with you. Your life is in San Francisco, so that's where we'll make ours together. Being with you is all that matters."

Her eyes sparkled as brightly as the diamond he'd picked out for her. Or maybe that was the reflection of his own. "I love you, too. I want to marry you, have a family with you. You are my life now. It doesn't matter where we live it," he pledged with a kiss.

She leaned against him and they started to walk again, as the clouds parted and the sun came out. "Then let's go home and dry off. And start living it."

Read on for a sneak peek of *Last Chance*, the
third installment in the
Chances Trilogy by Martha O'Sullivan, available
April 2021.

CHAPTER ONE

Last Chance

THE SHADE HADN'T BEEN in her sixty-four count, sharpener-inclusive box of crayons, but Moira Brody had known it for as long as she could remember. Saturating the winter sky, it hung behind the Sierra Nevadas like a ubiquitous curtain. The boundless blue haze framed the milky peaks and snow-laden pines before yielding to the preternatural liquid hue that was Lake Tahoe.

Moira's Sorel boots crunched on the snowpack as she welcomed the blast of fresh air replacing the arid closeness she'd been breathing for the last hour. Inhaling antidotally, she aimed her gait at the freshly shoveled path. She knocked and opened the door at the same time. "Linds?"

"Up here," answered a disembodied voice.

Moira stomped the snow off her boots, then shed them and her coat before following the sound of footfalls upstairs. The smell of fresh wood and lemon beeswax drew her to the bedroom at the end of the hall. There she found Lindsay Rembrandt contemplating three paint swatches taped to the wall.

"What do you think?" Lindsay asked without preamble, blonde ponytail swinging behind her. "Muted Mint, Seafoam Spray or Green Tea."

"You're the interior designer, not me." Moira walked over to the wall in question, drenched in bright winter sunshine. After a moment's consideration she replied mildly, "Muted Mint, not that it matters."

Lindsay immediately straightened her shoulders and knitted her brow. "Why wouldn't it matter?"

"Because," Moira answered, feeling the inner smile spread across her mouth. "When that baby girl is born, you're going to repaint. You should be looking at pink paint strips."

Lindsay's cobalt blue eyes narrowed with intrigue. "What makes you so sure it's a girl anyway?"

"Gut," she told her. "And you deserve a girl. You always wanted a sister."

"I thought I had one," Lindsay reminded her gently.

"You know what I mean." Moira returned the tender smile.

"Brian and I just want a healthy baby," she maintained, but the delight on her face intensified. "Besides, we already have Kelsey."

"Kelsey's nearly out of college. You could be a step-grandmother in a few years."

"Bite your tongue." Lindsay broke their shared gaze and reverted to the task at hand, giving Moira a profile view of her second trimester baby bump. "Good call with the Muted Mint, though. That's what we're painting the nursery at home. It seems silly to have one at each house, but I feel so close to Gram here. I want her to be a part of it."

"She'd be so happy for you, Linds. And so proud."

"I know." Lindsay brushed her fingertips across her damp lower lashes. "Damn hormones. I don't have a thing to cry about."

"Emily was the same way. And the cravings." Moira went on theatrically, waving her hand in the air. "Jack was forever running to Raley's in the middle of the night."

"How are the twins?"

"Great. I'm babysitting them on Friday night. They're starting to —"

"You're babysitting your nephews on Valentine's Day?" Spinning back around, Lindsay cut her off.

"Yeah."

"With Paul?"

"No."

"Why?"

"Because Jack and Emily hardly ever get an evening out, let alone an overnight."

"Why aren't you doing something with Paul on Valentine's Day?" Lindsay's tone was a mixture of disappointment and confusion.

Moira had wondered the same, but kept that to herself. "He hasn't mentioned anything. And you know how hard it is to find a babysitter on Valentine's Day." She hesitated, then added, "I offered."

"You offered?" Lindsay repeated in openmouthed wonder.

"Yeah, I stayed with the boys last year."

"But everything was different then!"

"It certainly was. They were barely walking. And you weren't married, let alone pregnant."

"I mean with you and Paul and you know it!"

Moira started with a tired breath. "Linds…"

"Did you break up?" Lindsay interjected.

"We didn't," Moira made air quotes with her fingers, "break up. We weren't really all the way together. "

Lindsay saw right through her. "You looked pretty together at my wedding."

"That was months ago," Moira reminded her.

"I knew something was up. You skirted the issue every time I brought it up. Shame on me for not putting two and two together sooner."

"Yeah, because between remodeling a house, going back to school and having a baby you should have been more on top of my love life. All while living four hours away."

Lindsay ignored Moira's sarcastic tone and came to her, taking her hands. "I didn't realize it was so…," she searched for the word, "casual between the two of you."

"Me neither." Moira's heart caught up with her mouth and she finished quietly, "It is what it is."

"And what is that exactly?"

"What it's always been. Friendship. Familiarity. History. Maybe that's all it's supposed to be," Moira told her with borrowed conviction.

"Maybe," Lindsay conceded with a skeptical squint.

"Now, show me the pink swatches you picked up."

Lindsay shot her a measured look, but took the hint. "You know me too well."

"Likewise," Moira replied, also knowing that the matter was far from laid to rest.

❧

"It's not like she owes me an explanation or anything," Paul Webster told Jack Brody later that afternoon. "I'm just surprised."

"I was too when she offered," Jack said from across his cluttered desk. "But I've learned not to ask too many questions of the women in my life. Beginning with my sister and ending with my wife."

Suddenly uncomfortable, Paul shifted in his seat and blew out a jagged breath. He'd gotten into the habit of taking Moira for granted, he supposed. But not to the tugging feeling in the pit of his stomach when he let himself think too much about her. "Where is she anyway?"

"Up at the lake. Lindsay's in town. They're picking out paint or curtains or something," Jack informed him with a dismissive wave.

"Figures."

"So what's the deal with you two anyway?" Jack tossed out pointedly. "Is it an on-again, off-again thing?"

"No." Paul found himself oddly offended. "There is no deal. It's Moira for God's sake. Sometimes it's just a little weird. Almost like dating your sister."

"Actually, it *is* dating my sister." Jack's hazel eyes clouded. "Don't break her heart or anything. Hate to say it, but blood is thicker than water. Even though you literally saved my life in the latter."

Jack ended on a high note, but Paul noted the nuance of his words. "It's not like that. We stumbled into I don't know what, and then right back out again. Hell, I'm in Portland nearly every week now and playing catch-up in the office on the weekends."

Jack silenced Paul's half-assed explanation with a decided hand. "Em figured I should talk to you before we made any definite Valentine's Day plans. In case you were planning a surprise."

Paul leaned forward in an attempt to settle the restlessness swirling inside him. "What kind of surprise?"

Jack shrugged. "Dinner, flowers, chocolates, little gifts. All that stuff I used to do before I got married."

Paul had done all that stuff too…for Lindsay, he reminded himself with a mental kick. But everything with Moira was different. Easy, casual, familiar. Wooing her didn't even occur to him. Should it? He sure as hell didn't like the idea of wooing her occurring to someone else.

"So can I tell my hopelessly romantic wife that we have a night to ourselves?" Jack's eyes danced hopefully.

"Only if she finds another babysitter," Paul decided out loud. "Moira has plans."

CHAPTER TWO

Last Chance

"HAPPY VALENTINE'S DAY."

Moira lifted her eyes from the computer monitor in the direction of the familiar voice.

"Happy Valentine's Day to you." She marked her place on the spreadsheet and pushed up from behind her desk. "I didn't expect to see you today."

"I was in the area unexpectedly. Thought I'd drop by my best account."

"Brody and Sons Construction is your best account, huh?" she challenged around a laugh.

"Okay," Jason Parker conceded affably. "My favorite account. I had a lunch meeting down the block." He took in the office asking, "Is Jack around?"

"Jack is never around on paydays or Friday afternoons. Today is both."

Jason's chiseled jaw relaxed, allowing his loose male grin to advertise his movie star-white teeth. "That's right. I've heard how your Irish temper comes out when you do the books."

"Small business ownership is a perpetual roller coaster. Business is strong but supply chain remains a challenge. It's a domino effect."

"Same here."

Moira returned the cordial, lingering smile, but intuition told her Jason had more than windows on his mind. And she wasn't sure how she felt about that. After a few silent beats she put in hurriedly, "I'll tell Jack you stopped by."

Jason didn't respond, only gave her a meditative nod. Then his expression tightened and Moira could almost see his heart begin to race inside his chest. "So, what are you up to tonight? Big Valentine's Day plans?" His blue eyes swept the office, then rested on Moira's desk as if searching for something.

Like flowers. Or a chocolate heart. Or anything to denote Valentine's Day.

Moira willed the heat rushing through her body not to settle in her cheeks. She cleared her throat and commended herself for having the inadvertent foresight to keep the reception desk between them. Then she answered in a voice higher than she would have liked. "Me? Oh, no. Someone has to keep the lights on around here, you know," she told him, gesturing to her desk. "And people expect to be paid, Valentine's Day or not."

That seemed to surprise, then please him. The confident countenance returned and rested squarely on the wide shoulders supporting his black suit coat. "How about dinner, then?

Everything decent is probably booked, but we could go a little later, after the rush," he offered with building enthusiasm. "That would give you time to finish up. Or we could get take-out and eat it here."

Grateful Jason didn't suggest take-out at his place, Moira began a weak internal debate. Her conversation with Paul the day before yesterday had been brief and in response to a butt call on his part. He hadn't said anything about Valentine's Day or the weekend. Emily had come down with the flu, so she and Jack were staying home. And Lindsay had gone back to San Francisco.

"You have to eat, one way or the other," Jason was still talking.

She met his expectant stare head-on. There was no reason not to accept his heartfelt invitation. "Take-out would be great," she decided out loud.

"Then it's a date," he triumphed. "Think about what you'd like to eat. I'll touch base in a few hours."

Moira pushed back the bittersweet twinges nipping at her stomach and managed an oblique smile. "Anything is fine. Surprise me."

❧

Paul mumbled under his breath and patted his pockets. He must have left his phone in the car. He cast his gaze upward, letting the sun's low position on the horizon confirm his suspicions that he was running late. The florist closed at six o'clock, Valentine's Day or not, he'd been told when placing his order. The clerk had also remarked that at this late juncture, his only saving grace was that he didn't want roses.

And that was not by accident.

He'd given Lindsay and every other woman he'd dated roses, but Moira was more of a hydrangea or a lily than a rose. Not that he'd ever given her flowers before, he self-admonished as that ineffable feeling began engulfing his gut again.

He picked up his pace and arrived at the florist in less than five minutes. The dry heat billowed out into the damp winter air the second he opened the shop door, biting at his cheeks. He got in line and began to mentally review his plan. Every restaurant in town was booked solid by the time he'd tried to make a reservation, but Moira was easy to please and take-out would surely due. The tricky part would be tearing her away from work so close to the fifteenth of the month.

He was ruminating on his midweek conversation with Jack for the umpteenth time when he heard an orotund voice behind him point out, "I think it's your turn."

Returning to the present, Paul threw an apology over his shoulder and stepped forward.

"No problem," the man returned. "I'm in no hurry myself, but the guy behind me is sweating bullets. Once you're in, you're in, I told him. Florists want to make money just like the rest of us."

Nodding in agreement, Paul turned his attention to the person addressing him from behind the counter.

"Picking up, sir?"

"Yeah. Webster."

The perky teenager punched at the keyboard and consulted the computer monitor. "One Spring Splash bouquet, substitute roses." She hit a few more keys, then handed Paul a receipt "They'll bring it right up."

Paul followed her silent direction and stepped aside. The customer behind him advanced and started with a sigh. "I know it's slim pickings, but are there any red roses left?"

"I'm sorry, sir," the girl apologized with the inklings of a smirk. "We're sold out of red roses, but have an array of other flowers. We could arrange something lovely for you."

Undaunted by what should be a less than startling revelation, the man rounded his cheeks conspiratorially. "Surely there must be something in the back? Even some imperfects? This is a first date; someone I've been interested in for a while. I don't want to blow it."

"We don't discount; the owner is very particular," she explained with a more compassionate smile. "But I could double-check the cuttings. You'll have to wait until I fill all these orders, though." She tipped her head at the dozen man deep line. "It might be a few minutes."

"No problem. She's working late anyway." He joined Paul next to the half empty glass door refrigerator. "I guess cuttings are better than nothing," he said around a shrug.

"I'm sure they'll find you something," Paul encouraged, feeling sorry for the complete stranger. "Might not be red roses though."

"I knew that would be a long shot."

"I wish I could have given you mine. I had them switched out."

"You're kidding," he returned with a jolt. "What woman doesn't like roses? Especially on Valentine's Day?"

"It's not that she wouldn't like them. They just don't suit her."

The man laughed without opening his mouth. "For your sake I hope not."

Just then another clerk appeared from behind the counter calling, "Mr. Webster?"

"Right here."

Stepping forward, Paul took the cellophane wrapped bouquet from the young woman's hands. "Thanks."

"My pleasure."

Turning around, he shot his new acquaintance a tight nod. "Good luck."

"Same to you."

Suddenly dismayed by the thought that he would need it, Paul turned on his heel and walked out into the brisk night. It was full dark now and the headlights gleaming off the wet pavement reminded him of his next stop. He wondered if Moira would be as surprised to receive the gift as he'd been to buy it. But he'd felt as compelled to purchase it as he had been to be with her tonight. He'd held up his part of the deal, whatever the deal was. The rest was up to her.

CHAPTER THREE

Last Chance

MOIRA PUSHED HER SIDE-SWEPT bangs out of her eyes and expelled her third calming breath. She'd flown through payroll before running home to change and freshen up. Now she was back at the office with the intention of reconciling the ledgers. Instead she was contemplating herself in the full-length mirror on the back of the bathroom door for a least the fifth time.

She hadn't wanted to wear the distressed jeans and cotton sweater she'd thrown on this morning, but didn't want to try too hard either. A dress was out of the question and presumptuous, not that she had anything appropriate anyway. So she'd chosen the floral blouse she'd bought on her last trip to San Francisco and skinny jeans with a little bling on the back pockets. The outfit had been easy; the shoes were the problem. She looked from one foot to the other, each modeling an option. Boots were casual and sexy. Heels were stylish and sexy. Both sent a message—a sexy one. But Moira wasn't sure sexy was the message she wanted to send.

She hadn't had a date, first or otherwise, in ages. Lindsay's wedding had been as close to a real date as Paul and she had gotten, Moira supposed.

Other than that it was going here and there, seeing a movie, attending an event or a family function. None of which were ever followed by anything more than a parting good night kiss.

Except for that night.

That kiss, or kisses, she corrected herself, had been the first time there'd been anything more. The first time the yank in her stomach had crept downward and settled between her thighs. The first time the buzzing in her head had spread to every cell in her body and exploded. The first time the steady canter of her heartbeat became a hastening gallop. But not the first time Paul had backed off and said good night. That happened every time.

Not that she would have wanted to lose her virginity in such a wine-induced state anyway, she grunted under her breath. And to all people, Paul Webster, her ninth grade lab partner and brother's best friend.

Yes she did, she thought, grimacing at her reflection.

But of late Paul had been aloof, indifferent, busy. And in Portland half the time.

Jason Parker, however, the ash-blond, spring ski-tanned, five o'clock-shadowed window salesman was in her office every other week. With biceps as wide and eyes as bright as the Squaw Valley slopes. And he seemed genuinely excited about spending the evening with her. And not just any evening.

Valentine's Day. A Valentine's Day date. Jason had said so himself.

Her thoughts were returning to her footwear dilemma when she heard the door chimes ring. "Shit!" she swore under her breath, pushing down the melancholy. She kicked off the chunky heel and tugged on the other pump boot, then indulged herself with another quick glance in the mirror. Scrunching the teeming curls she'd grown up hating, she squared her shoulders and painted on a smile.

But when Moira emerged with a cheery greeting on her lips, she found the office just as empty as she had left it. Except for the artfully arranged bouquet of red roses cradled in white carnations sitting on the counter. She discharged a shotgun breath. This was definitely a date. The rosebuds were small and the stems short, peeking out of the hourglass-shaped vase girdled with a red velvet bow. She was leaning down to sniff one when she realized Jason was standing in the doorway. Shuffling back a step, she threw an alarmed hand to her chest. "Oh! I didn't see you there."

He took the two remaining steps to complete his entry and approached her. "Sorry. I didn't mean to startle you. I dropped those off and ran back out to the car for the food." His appreciative gaze took her in from head to toe. "Happy Valentine's Day, Moira. You look incredible."

"Thanks," she returned. "You too."

He'd traded his suit and tie for a casual shirt and the dress pants for slim-fitting jeans. He was standing within a few breaths of her now with a blank look on his face, seemingly debating something.

Like kissing her.

Admittedly only partly relieved when he didn't, she shifted her gaze back to the flowers. "The roses are beautiful. Thank you."

"My pleasure. And my second lucky break of the day," he told her. "By the time I got to the florist, they were already sold out. I talked the clerk into selling me the day's cuttings."

How sweet, Moira thought. That sounded like something Paul would do.

For Lindsay.

She cleared the past from her throat. "I bet they were slammed."

"As advertised. So was Bernini's." He raised his arms to the elbows, displaying two brown paper bags. "I took the safe route with Italian. Hope that's okay."

"Perfect. I haven't eaten all day. Where do you want to sit?" she asked, gesturing around the room with her hand. "We don't really have an eating area. Just a kitchenette in the back."

He gave the office an appraising glance, then rested his gaze on the desk in the corner. "Want to pull up a couple of chairs over there?"

The desk was in abeyance, but cleared off thanks to Lindsay and her temporary insanity. Being Paul's biggest fan, she'd be furious to know it went to such use. Moira snickered to herself. "Sure."

"So, did you get the books done?" Jason asked, removing his leather jacket and hanging it on the back of the chair. A woodsy, ginger spice scent wafted through the air and formed a steady current under Moira's nose.

"Almost," she answered as they doled out the foiled-covered containers. "Payroll is sent and that's the most important thing. I can always reconcile over the weekend."

His eyes filled with understanding and she could almost see the wheels turning in his head. "Do you work a lot on the weekends?"

Moira started with a sigh. "Lately it seems. First world problems. How about you?"

"Yeah. Paperwork, paperwork. Or should I say paperless work? But either way, I'd rather be skiing or boarding." His voice trailed off and he pulled two wine bottles out of the second bag. "Which do you prefer?"

"Skiing," she told him, relaxing a little. "My eye-foot coordination is better than my sense of balance."

Chuckling, he glanced down. "I'll keep that in mind. But I meant red or white?" He displayed a bottle of each.

Moira felt her cheeks burst into flame. "Oh," she faltered. "Red would be great. Do you need a corkscrew? I think there's one back there."

"No," Jason declined, pulling out one. "Got that covered. Just some glasses."

"Sure."

Complying, Moira started to walk away, until Jason caught her arm and professed, "I'm really glad you agreed to have dinner with me, especially tonight. I was almost afraid to ask."

"I'm glad you did," Moira affirmed after a long moment, hoping she sounded more sincere than she felt inside. He really was a nice guy. She left him with a closemouthed smile and headed for the kitchen.

All she could find was plastic cups, but they would have to do. She considered bringing out the candles they kept around for emergencies, but thought better of it. She didn't want to come on too strong and give Jason the wrong impression. And no matter how hard she tried, she couldn't get Paul out of her mind. What was he doing tonight, she wondered?

So when she returned to the front a few minutes later and found him just inside the threshold of the door, she blinked hard a couple of times, thinking it was her imagination. There was that split second of consternation and joy as she watched him stand there, rooted in pie-eyed wonder, slicing his astonished stare between Jason and her.

It was a good thing Solo cups were all Moira could find, because they immediately fell through her splaying fingers. They struck the tile floor, one clangorous bounce at a time, then rolled away. Frozen in the inertia of utter disbelief, she could only let them go and bring a shocked hand to her mouth. It took her three reflective blinks to process the flowers in Paul's left hand, the bottle of wine in his right. Then her prickling eyes reunited with his caramel-colored ones. His were stormy, full of confusion and awe. And bygone scars.

Guilty satisfaction juxtaposed the shock and wound into a tight braid of angst in her stomach. Finally after a few interminable beats, she stammered, "Paul. What are you doing here?"

"I could ask you the same question," Paul replied derisively.

There was a long, heavy silence during which Moira fought an overwhelming urge to run away.

She was still striving for calm when she heard Jason clear his throat uneasily and announce, "I'll just go grab some napkins from the back."

With a grateful nod Moira waited for him leave, then addressed Paul loftily. "I'm having dinner."

"I can see that." His voice clipped. "With whom?"

"A friend."

Paul's sable brows furrowed suspiciously. "I don't know him."

"You don't know all my friends," she told him with a superior air.

"Obviously."

"Besides, he's a new friend."

"Dinner with a new friend. On Valentine's Day," he chided. "How quaint."

"I didn't have any other plans, did I?" Her voice suddenly sounded more pitiful than she would have liked.

Stretched beyond his usually level limit, Paul's posture stiffened and he closed the distance between them with three calculated strides. "What kind of a friend is he?" he demanded as the smell of anise replaced its outdoorsy predecessor.

"Just a friend," she told him with an assumptive shrug, noticing for the first time that he was dressed up.

"Then what am I?"

There was a moment so quiet Moira could hear static crackling in the air. Finally she broke it. "I don't know. A friend I've hardly seen or spoken to much lately."

Paul's expression softened a little, like he already knew that. And it bothered him.

"I see. So how long have you and..."

"Jason," Moira finished for him, trying to ignore the familiar, intoxicating scent filling the small space between them.

"Jason," he began again, "been friends?"

"He's called on us for the last year or two."

"Ah, so he's a work friend? No wonder," Paul disdained. "He wouldn't know that you don't like the sauce at Bernini's. It's too sweet." He shifted his gaze to the salad Jason had started doling out. "And that you don't care for black olives."

Moira raised her chin a notch. "I can pick them off. And no, he wouldn't know that. It's our first date," she countered briskly.

"So it *is* a date?" Paul returned to her with flinty eyes and a corded neck. "A first date on Valentine's Day. Sweet," he mocked. "And to think I was worried about tearing you away from your spreadsheets in the middle of the month."

"Tear me away for what?" she couldn't help but ask.

"Dinner, for starters." Flippant now, he consulted the TAG Heuer on his wrist. "It should be here anytime." Then his regard settled on the multicolored bouquet in his hand, as if just remembering he was holding it. He deliberated for a few seconds before setting it on her desk with a resounding thud. "I'll leave these here, seeing how the front counter is crowded."

Had that bulging vein below his right temple always been there? "Paul—"

"I'll hang on to the Cakebread, though," he plowed over her. "It's too good of a year to waste."

He started for the door, but turned on his heel mid-stride to face her again. "Funny. I never pegged you for roses. Too ostentatious. But I guess I was wrong about that too. Happy Valentine's Day, Moira."

The braid in her stomach unwound into a strands of dread as she watched him swing the door open and storm out into the night. Beside herself, she could only stand there in stunned silence, hand clasped at her breastbone and tears stinging her eyes.

"Is it safe to come out now?" came a tentative voice from somewhere in the back.

Suddenly remembering Jason was here, she spun around in complete mortification. "Yes, of course. I'm so sorry. We just had a little... miscommunication."

"Sounds like more than that to me," Jason contended mildly. "Maybe I should go."

"No!" she exclaimed in short order. "Please don't. This is all so lovely. I'd really like you to stay. I mean..." She wrung her hands. "If you still want to. But I understand if you don't."

"I do," he told her quietly, then approached her with eyes full of trepidation. "I just don't want to get in the way."

"You couldn't." Moira noted the weight of his words and shaking her head slowly from side to side, matched it. "Because there isn't anything to get in the way of."

CHAPTER FOUR

Last Chance

THE BLACK ICE CAST an eerie sheen on the road ahead and the glare of the oncoming high beams had Paul squinting as if at the summer sun. The weather was coming in fast and he wondered if Moira had gotten home safely.

Or alone.

Or at all.

He should've gotten her roses. But he didn't. Because she's Moira. Effortlessly beautiful, remarkably grounded, perpetually good-natured Moira. And tonight she was something else— incredibly sexy. In tight-fitting jeans and a silky top he'd never seen before. With her thick, voluminous, begging to be touched curls skimming her shoulders. And eye makeup and red lipstick. She smelled pretty good too. Like spring rain and lilacs.

All for the guy begging for roses at the flower shop. For someone he'd been "interested in" for a while. For whom he had a last minute arrangement thrown together. From *his* cuttings. For *his* girl. Paul huffed out a harried breath. Is that what she was? Apparently not. But he sure as hell wanted her to be. He slammed on the brakes and the SUV swerved, then leveled, sliding into the precarious U-turn.

It took Paul twice as long as usual to get back to Reno with the slick roads. And by then the temperature had dipped enough to turn the spitting rain into steely pellets. A frigid, damp sleet akin to the block of ice that had staked a claim in the pit of his stomach.

Turning the corner of Moira's street, he heaved a half-hearted sigh of relief when he saw no car in the driveway and a hodgepodge of lights burning inside. She was home. Alone it would seem.

Unless they came in one car, he prepared himself through gritted teeth.

Paul knew the garage code, but didn't want to scare her, so he opted for the conventional route. He could see her profile through the slats of the plantation shutters as he made his way up the path to the front porch. She was in the kitchen fussing with something, still dressed up like she hadn't been home long.

His throat muscles contracted as his mind began to race. Had her date seen her home or had they parted ways at the office? Gone somewhere for a drink after dinner? Made another date? He looked on as Moira stepped back from the kitchen island, arms drawn across her chest, and appraised her work. The fancy jeans sat just below her hips, hugging every one of her curves from hip to ankle and Paul found himself disturbingly covetous. The sheer shirt rested on her slim waist and reminded him of holding her in his arms when they danced at Lindsay's wedding. And her breasts looked bigger somehow, like they'd grown overnight. The mere thought of touching them made his heart skip a beat and his cock begin to swell.

Seemingly pleased with her work, she reached for the dish towel flung over her shoulder and dried her hands, catching a glimpse of him out of the corner of her eye. She did a double take, then held his perceptive gaze momentarily. He thought the corners of her mouth curved slightly upward, but the distance between them was too great to be sure. She shook off whatever she was thinking and walked toward the front door. He visualized her on the other side, squeezing her eyes shut and taking a few deep breaths before opening it. She greeted him with a wobbly, "Hey."

She looked captivating in the amber light. Her emerald green eyes were soft and clung to his as if unwittingly attached. Her full lips were naked now and Paul told himself it was from eating. The coal-black tendrils had doubled, the errant strands falling in sexy waves around her fair face. Also from natural causes, he told himself. "Hey. Can I come in?"

"Of course," she invited, ushering him in.

Stepping inside, Paul rapid-fired, "I'm glad you're home. I wanted to—"

"Where else would I be at eleven o'clock at night?" she cut him off.

"I don't know." His mind was suddenly a mare's nest and his palms were beginning to sweat. "I wasn't sure what your plans were for the rest of the evening."

"I've been home for almost an hour," she informed him crisply.

"Alone?" His eyes scanned the house beckoningly.

"Yes," Moira patronized. "It was just dinner, Paul."

On Valentine's Day, he silently added. "About that, I came by to apologize." He wondered if she sensed the audible relief in his voice. "I shouldn't have assumed we'd see each other tonight. And I certainly shouldn't have assumed you'd be," he bit off the word, "available." He looked away then, into the kitchen, and saw what she'd been doing. Arranging flowers.

His flowers.

She must have acquired clairvoyant powers in those few seconds, because her tone softened and she said, "I had to bring them home. They were too beautiful to waste."

Like her.

With four wide steps he advanced into the kitchen and gave it a cursory once-over. "Where are the roses?"

She followed him. "At the office."

"They're not too beautiful to waste?" he asked in a thick voice, turning to face her.

"No, they are." Her breath hitched. "They're just not from you."

Her eyes, soulful now, were filling behind their dark lashes and she was biting her bottom lip, trying to hold back the tears. Paul couldn't have stopped himself from going to her if he'd wanted to.

"Moira, what are we doing?" he implored, gripping her forearms. "What have I done? Have I lost you?"

She shook her head from side to side and the tears began to fall, leaving sooty tracks on her cheeks. Tipping his head back in silent thanks, Paul gathered her in his arms. She instantly moved into his body, sniffling through sawed-off breaths.

"Tell me nothing happened. Tell me there's nothing between you and him," he prayed out loud after a long moment.

She answered by burrowing her head into his shoulder and wreathing his middle. He felt her breathing level off and he kissed the top of her head. She smelled like a subtle version of earlier, infused with wine and garlic. Hope replaced the uneasiness in his stomach and he heard himself say, "I had to force myself not to go back there. I've been driving around for hours, going crazy."

She angled out of his grasp just enough to make eye contact. Suddenly she was the girl he used to know again, not the woman tying his insides into knots. Or maybe the perfect combination of both. Her eyes began to shine and a satisfied smile curved her lips. "You have?"

"Yeah. Like outside my mind crazy." He laid his lips on hers and tasted the salt from her tears. She melted into the kiss, then the next. He wondered if she could sense him growing behind the zipper. Or the spool of want unwinding into a thousand frazzled threads in his gut. Gasping for air, he released her mouth and cupped her face. "You make me crazy, Moira Brody. Absolutely crazy."

Her breath caught in her throat and she swallowed hard and said, "Then I like you crazy."

Resting his forehead on hers, he let the night roll off his back like sweat. Then he closed his eyes and asked, "Do I need to fight for you, Moira?"

She laughed a little. "Well, Jason did bring flowers, dinner, wine."

"I brought flowers, dinner, wine," Paul defended high-mindedly, straightening. "Did you ever get the Chinese food?"

"Yeah, it's in there." She nodded over his shoulder at the sub-zero they'd picked out together.

"It's your favorite. Cashew chicken."

"Thank God," she said lightly, dabbing the outer corners of her eyes. "I'm starving."

Paul sent her a confused look. "Did Bernini's have a bad night?"

"Not from what I picked at."

"Poor guy," he gloated through a chuckle. "Went to all that trouble for nothing."

"I wouldn't say for nothing," Moira demurred, her eyes dancing with innuendo. "He seemed to enjoy the evening."

"Oh?" inquired Paul, stepping out of her embrace.

Gleaming now, she raised her eyebrows mischievously. "Yeah."

He felt his expression fall. "Did he kiss you good night?"

"He did," preened Moira.

Paul couldn't believe how much that bothered him. "Did you want him to?"

Her face instantly sobered. "No," she paused, then finished with hushed care. "I wanted you to come back."

"I did." As if he'd had any choice in the matter. Paul drew her to him again and ran his hands up and down her back. "I had to."

"That was all I could think about during dinner," she admitted into the crook of his shoulder. "That I could've spent Valentine's Day with you."

"It's not over quite yet." He leaned back and dried her tearstained cheeks with his thumbs. "Think he'll call you?"

She shrugged matter-of-factly. "Yeah."

"What will you say?"

"What should I say?"

"Thanks, but no thanks." He reached into his jacket pocket.

Her eyes narrowed as she took the small box from his open hands. "Paul, what is this?"

He gestured toward the bow-topped lid with a tip of the head. "Open it and find out."

Moira obliged as Paul looked on eagerly. A tiny gasp escaped her throat when she saw the diamond studs inside.

"I know they're on the small side, but you're not one for flash."

She glided her fingertips over each diamond. "They're beautiful."

"Emily thought they were perfect." Just like you, he almost said.

Her astonished gaze shifted upward. "Emily?"

"She's not sick. She found another sitter for tonight." He paused to let the benevolent betrayal sink in. "So we could spend Valentine's Day together."

"Oh, Paul! I'm so sorry!" Moira exclaimed. "I had no idea."

Neither did he. Until just now. And the realization hit him like a ton of bricks. "You can make it up to me tomorrow night," he told her on the fly. "We're going on a date. It'll be our first one."